MY NAME IS IRON EYES

Riding his palomino stallion, Iron Eyes escorts Squirrel Sally's stagecoach through the town of Lobo. The infamous bounty hunter is weary, and the remote settlement seems a peaceful place to rest — but Iron Eyes is mistaken. As he steers his mount down the main street, his eyes light upon a row of tethered horses. His instincts flare when he realises that the black roan with the white-tipped tail belongs to Buffalo Jim McCoy, a fearsome outlaw worth five thousand dollars — dead or alive . . .

Books by Rory Black
in the Linford Western Library:

THE FURY OF IRON EYES
THE WRATH OF IRON EYES
THE CURSE OF IRON EYES
THE SPIRIT OF IRON EYES
THE GHOST OF IRON EYES
IRON EYES MUST DIE
THE BLOOD OF IRON EYES
THE REVENGE OF IRON EYES
IRON EYES MAKES WAR
IRON EYES IS DEAD
THE SKULL OF IRON EYES
THE SHADOW OF IRON EYES
THE VENOM OF IRON EYES
IRON EYES THE FEARLESS
THE SCARS OF IRON EYES
A ROPE FOR IRON EYES
THE HUNT FOR IRON EYES

RORY BLACK

MY NAME IS IRON EYES

Complete and Unabridged

LINFORD
Leicester

First published in Great Britain in 2014 by
Robert Hale Limited
London

First Linford Edition
published 2016
by arrangement with
Robert Hale
an imprint of The Crowood Press
Wiltshire

A catalogue record for this book is available from the British Library.

ISBN 978–1–4448–2966–2

Published by
F. A. Thorpe (Publishing)
Anstey, Leicestershire

Set by Words & Graphics Ltd.
Anstey, Leicestershire
Printed and bound in Great Britain by
T. J. International Ltd., Padstow, Cornwall

This book is printed on acid-free paper

*Dedicated to the memory
of my little brave friend
Dylan Morgan-Ward.*

Prologue

The fiery sun was sinking inevitably into the quicksand of night. The sky was on fire. Scarlet tapers of defiant rays scarred the heavens as slowly stars began to appear like diamonds across the vast expanse of sky. Like everything else in the untamed territory nothing died easy in these parts, not even the last throes of day. It was as though the gods were battling with one another. The gods of day against the deities of night were forging their daily rituals. A devilish hue lit up the vast landscape which surrounded the small town. Every tree and cactus shimmered with the glowing crimson light cast down from the blood-coloured sky.

Yet this transition from day into night would prove to be different from all those that had gone before. The war that nature was displaying with all of its usual grandeur would prove to be something more than just a vibrant sunset this time.

It would prove to be a warning to look at what was heading towards the remote settlement at breakneck pace. For the true danger was not above the wooden shingled rooftops but on the dusty ground.

For the majority of townsfolk it was just the end of another day, like so many others, but to those who could read the signs this was an omen. An omen of impending peril which was about to occur in the midst of the remote settlement, called simply Lobo. Within hours nothing would ever be the same again. The colour of the sky would soon be spread across the dusty streets of Lobo in the form of blood.

No one knew it as the sun started to disappear behind the distant rocks, but death was coming. The blood of men both good and bad would soon be spilled.

The last rays of the forest fire glowed

defiantly above the small town as though the Devil himself were about to make an appearance.

In a strange way that was exactly what was about to happen. For there were many creatures said to have been created in the bowels of Hell. Some cast in human form. These were not pointed-tailed crimson monsters but actual men who seemed to walk and talk as all men do.

Yet there was something very different about those who seemed to have been manufactured by the demonic hands of Satan himself. They stood apart and oozed danger from every pore of their rancid bodies.

Some men are branded as less than human from their earliest days of life and grow into the monsters they are portrayed to be. They learn to accept the prejudice that their strange appearances bestow.

Yet all are all dangerous.

The infamous Iron Eyes had been called many things since his skeletal being had first emerged from the depths of the forests a dozen years earlier. Nothing about him seemed to fit into the realms of civilization.

There was no place for a misfit even in a land filled with misfits.

He looked unlike any other man in what was known as the Wild West. He was an outcast carved from the wood of an unknown tree. His long black hair draped his shoulders like a cape. The matted strands hid the brutal scars that had mutilated his features until they no longer even appeared to belong to a living man.

Every battle was carved into his face.

Some said he was an Indian and yet no tribe claimed him as one of their own. They hated him for some strange reason that none of them could articulate. To them he was an evil spirit, which had to be destroyed.

Iron Eyes fared no better in the minds and souls of the white men he encountered. They also feared the strange-looking bounty hunter.

Some believed he was the unholy offspring of a hideous liaison between a feral woman and the Devil. That he was a cruel mistake, doomed to wander the wastes of the vast West until somehow he managed to return to the cesspit from which he had been spawned.

Many seemed convinced that Iron Eyes was not even alive, for no matter how many horrendous injuries his tall, thin body sustained he never died from any of his them.

Was he, as so many men of all colours believed, nothing more than a ghost? Was Iron Eyes already dead and that was the reason why no one had as yet been able to stop his relentless progress?

A thousand stories had been told of the creature known simply as Iron Eyes. Some of the most brutal were true. Even those who had never even set eyes upon his emaciated form had heard of him. His name and description had spread like a cancer throughout the land he roamed.

Since he had turned his lethal skill with his pair of Navy Colt handguns to hunting wanted men for the bounty on their heads, Iron Eyes had become feared more than any other bounty hunter.

For once he had your Wanted poster buried deep in his trail-coat pocket, it was said that you were as good as dead. For Iron Eyes never quit his hunting and would keep trailing his chosen prey to the ends of the earth until he had you in his sights.

Then he would kill you mercilessly. For wanted dead or alive meant only one thing to Iron Eyes.

It meant dead.

For years he had hunted like a rabid wolf. Shunned and alone he did what few other men would even dare to do. He would risk everything and hunt down notorious outlaws with bounty money on their heads.

Years of hunting outlaws had only reinforced his own belief that he was different from all other two-legged creatures. He had begun to believe the stories which haunted him that he was to live and die alone.

Iron Eyes was the only one of his breed.

Unlike Adam he had never had an Eve.

A few months earlier he had stumbled across a massacre of innocents. The young daughter of the slaughtered family had survived and decided to travel with the then wounded Iron Eyes. Sally Cooke was more than a match for the thin bounty hunter and seemed to be blind to his scarred appearance and deaf to the stories others branded him with.

Unlike most grown men in the untamed West Iron Eyes had no knowledge of females and did not understand them. For the most part the feminine gender had steered clear of the monstrous-looking bounty hunter, but not Squirrel Sally.

She alone saw beyond the scars. She alone saw deep inside the strange, unique being, and not only liked what she had discovered but wanted it.

Sally was the only person whom Iron Eyes was actually afraid of, because she did not turn her eyes away from his monstrous features. Young as she was, the feisty youngster had the notorious bounty hunter roped. No matter how hard he tried to escape her advances Squirrel Sally could not be shaken off.

She refused to accept rejection or defeat. Iron Eyes belonged to her whether he liked it or not, or whether he even knew it or not.

The ground in and around Lobo began to shudder in answer to the pounding of the advancing horses' hoofs.

The last of the town's street lanterns had been lit as the sky darkened to reveal a thousand stars. A glowing line of amber light stretched out through the streets of the remote settlement like a chain of fireflies. The almost orange hue of burning coal tar danced off the array of wooden buildings and the shoulders of the town's inhabitants. The coming of nightfall meant little to most of the people who lived within the confines of such towns. Most did not even seem to notice the transition from day to night.

Then the sound of a cracking bullwhip resounded around the small town of Lobo as Sally steered the six-horse team of her stagecoach into the wide main street. Riding beside the coach upon his palomino stallion, Iron Eyes sat hunched over his ornate saddle horn, tapping his spurs with each beat of his heart.

Iron Eyes saw everything that moved as he led the long vehicle deep into the very soul of Lobo.

The faces of the townsfolk looked at the haunting rider and the battle-weary stagecoach as it thundered past them and headed deep into the heart of the town.

Lobo was smaller than most towns but it had everything a visitor might need. Places to eat, drink and sleep. It also had a well-illuminated sheriff's office set midway along the main street.

As his bullet-coloured eyes darted from behind the veil of long, limp strands of black hair Iron Eyes studied each and every face they focused upon. If any of the faces he briefly glanced at were wanted the most notorious bounty hunter west of the Pecos would have instantly known it. Yet to his surprise none of them were recognizable.

'Relax, Iron Eyes,' Sally shouted down from the driver's board of the stagecoach.

'It don't pay to relax, Squirrel.' Iron Eyes spat as he dragged a cigar from his battered coat pocket and rammed it between his razor-sharp teeth. 'Men die easy when they're relaxed.'

'You fret too much,' the female joked.

'Yep. I always do when I'm clean out of whiskey, gal.'

She watched as the rider ignited a match with his thumbnail and cupped its flame in his hands. Smoke trailed over his wide, lean shoulders.

'I thought you was out of cigars.' Sally leaned down, snatched the cigar from his mouth and rammed it between her dry lips.

Iron Eyes glanced up at the youngster and then exhaled a line of smoke. 'I am now, Squirrel.'

The sound of the stagecoach team's chains echoed off the weathered buildings as they passed. A chain gang of a hundred shackled prisoners could not have equalled the haunting noise.

Iron Eyes drew rein and slowed his tall stallion as he neared a saloon with its light cascading out into the street ahead of them. He looked back as Squirrel Sally pushed her bare foot down on the brake pole and pulled her hefty reins up to her chin.

The stallion stopped. Iron Eyes swung the horse around and watched through narrowed eyes as the youngster managed expertly to stop the six-horse team a few inches away from his mount.

'Why'd you stop here, sweetheart?'

Sally called down through a cloud of smoke.

Iron Eyes tapped his spurs and rode to beneath the high driver's perch. He halted his horse and looked up at her.

'I ain't sure, Squirrel,' he replied.

'Did you spot someone?' Sally asked as she looped the reins around the pole. 'Did you see an outlaw with bounty on his head? Did you?'

Iron Eyes ran his bony fingers through his mane of long hair and looked back along the street down which they had just travelled.

'I saw something,' he replied.

'What did you see?'

'I ain't sure.' The bounty hunter wrapped his long leathers around his saddle horn and steadied his mount with his thin legs. His hands reached down into the bullet-filled pockets of his trail coat and pulled out the deadly pair of matched Navy Colts.

Sally puffed on the cigar between her lips and stood on the driver's board. She squinted hard down into the lantern-lit street.

'All I see is a bunch of lathered-up saddle horses tied to hitching rails back there,' she remarked. 'All the folks we drove past have up and gone.'

The words made the deadly horseman take his eyes off his weaponry and raise his head. His scarred eyebrows rose.

'That's it,' he muttered.

Sally shrugged. 'That's what, Bacon Britches?'

'Horses,' Iron Eyes repeated. 'A bunch of horses.'

The infuriated female sighed and sucked hard on the cigar. 'You might not have noticed but this damn street is full of horses, Iron Eyes. What's so damn interesting about the ones back there?'

The bounty hunter pushed one of his guns into his belt until its grip nestled against his buckle. He cocked the hammer of the other.

'Didn't you notice the black roan with the white tip to its tail, Squirrel?'

Iron Eyes asked, a cruel smile etching itself across his hideous features. 'There's only one horse like that that I know about in this whole territory. Buffalo Jim McCoy's.'

'What in tarnation are you jabbering about?' Sally asked as she drew in the last of the cigar's smoke. 'So what does it matter if there's only one black roan in this territory? Are you figuring on killing it just because it belongs to some outlaw?'

Iron Eyes stood in his stirrups as his left hand unwrapped his reins from the saddle horn. He balanced for a few seconds in his stirrups with one of his deadly six-shooters gripped firmly in his hand.

'Buffalo Jim McCoy owns it and he's worth five thousand bucks dead or alive, gal,' Iron Eyes informed his young companion. 'That's why.'

Before Sally could say another word the bounty hunter had whipped the shoulders of his stallion and thundered back along the street towards the line of horses. She sat down and spat the cigar at the sand.

'Ten more yards and we'd have reached the saloon,' she murmured, and sighed.

1

Ten hours earlier a new dawn had blistered the flesh of the five horsemen as they steered their lathered-up mounts through the unrelenting heat of the vast desolation towards the distant town known simply as Lobo. Clouds of dust rose up into the heavens but none of the riders slowed their pace. They had ridden a long way to reach this place at this time. These were not drifters but men who had purpose.

They had passed the scarred landscape without even turning their heads to look at the ravaged terrain. To them silver mines meant nothing but loot. None of the quintet of horsemen had ever done a hard day's toil in his life and none of them ever would.

They had other ideas.

To them, the miners broke their backs and worked hard whilst they reaped the profits by any means possible. At the head of the riders, seated astride his magnificent black roan, the most calculating of their bunch led his small gang towards their goal.

Buffalo Jim McCoy was one of those outlaws who had become a legend over the past ten years, yet he had only struck three times during that period, each time with increasing brutality. For McCoy was one of that rare breed of outlaw who chose to disappear into the large cities after his work had been done and rub shoulders with the more affluent.

Not for him the constant roaming and hiding from the law in between his lucrative strikes. McCoy chose to take on the façade of a gentleman and to show that all a man required was money.

But the rider's journey to Lobo was obstructed.

Buffalo Jim McCoy reined in his black roan. His brooding eyes studied what was before them. His newly recruited gang stopped their mounts beside the more experienced McCoy and wondered what he would do.

Dust drifted from the hoofs of the five mounts as their masters watched the group of miners who blocked the road to and from Lobo.

'What them miners doing, Buffalo?' Tom Brown asked his leader. He pulled the brim of his hat down to shield his eyes from the blinding rays of the rising sun.

Buffalo placed a cigar between his teeth and watched the seven miners. Each of them was armed with a pickaxe. He blew smoke away from them and then rested a gloved hand on the horn of his saddle. There was deadly determination in the outlaw leader and it showed. He alone knew what to do when confronted by trouble.

Buffalo turned his head and stared through the cigar smoke at his four hand-picked followers.

'I've heard that some of these miners

get skittish when their payroll is due,' he answered drily.

'What do you mean, Buffalo?' another of the riders, named Doyle, asked. 'How come they're skittish?'

Buffalo twisted on his saddle and stared with cold, deadly eyes at his men. They were all shy of his thirty-seven years and it showed.

'These men ain't like us, boys. They're a special breed of critter. They work hard and every month or so they get paid,' Buffalo explained. 'Then when they've got their wages in their hands they go and spend the whole bundle on women and drink in record time.'

'Then what do they do?' Brown asked.

'They knuckle down and start working again,' Buffalo replied through a cloud of cigar smoke. 'Seems pointless to me.'

Another of the five riders pointed at the group of miners. 'What are they doing, blocking the road like that? Do they think we'll quit riding into Lobo?'

Buffalo gave a slow nod. 'I reckon so. Them boys are damn ornery and no mistake.'

'What'll we do?' Denver Short asked, moving his mount next to the black roan.

A curious expression carved its way across the face of the rider of the black roan. He was surprised by the question.

'We kill them,' Buffalo Jim McCoy spat. 'What else?'

Like a troop of cavalry the four horsemen drove their mounts through the arid landscape and followed their leader towards the hostile miners. When they were within fifty or so feet of the human barricade the outlaws followed Buffalo's lead and drew their weaponry.

McCoy drove his sturdy mount straight through the miners and then swung his black roan around. He aimed his six-shooter and squeezed its trigger.

A thunderstorm could not have created more noise.

White lightning spewed from every

barrel. Deadly shots of hot lead traced through the dry air down into the miners who had tried to stop their progress. One by one each of the miners crumpled into a heap of scarlet gore. Those who had not died from the bullets that had ripped through their bodies were trampled under the hoofs of the five riders. Buffalo was not satisfied just to see all of the seven miners fall to the ground. He continued to fire his guns down into their already stricken bodies.

It soon became evident that this had not just been senseless murder.

This had been a slaughter on a grand scale.

This was nothing more than an execution.

Only when Buffalo had been certain that every one of the miners were dead did he stop firing his guns. Smoke billowed unchecked from the hot gun barrels of each of their weapons before Buffalo raised a hand.

He sat silently astride his mount,

smiling as his long thin fingers pulled fresh shells from his gunbelt. He shook the spent casings from his gun before sliding fresh bullets into each of the six chambers.

'Drag them corpses out of sight, boys,' he ordered his men. 'We don't want anyone in Lobo to know what we've just done. They might get ideas.'

Only the red stains on the sand gave any clue as to what had happened after the five riders had continued on their journey towards the unsuspecting town.

Like a military general at the head of a cavalry charge Buffalo Jim McCoy led his men down into Lobo.

* * *

The magnificent palomino obeyed its master and drew to an abrupt halt beside the line of tethered saddle horses. Iron Eyes held the Navy Colt at his chest as his eyes darted all around the area. The building behind the hitching rail was a store of some kind that the lethal bounty hunter knew had nothing to do with the five resting horses. Iron Eyes looped a long thin leg over the head of the stallion and then slid to the ground.

Every one of his honed hunting instincts warned him to be careful as he led his mount to the end of the line of horses. He tied his reins to the twisted pole and moved closer to the nervous horses.

Unlike his own mount the animals shied. They could smell the scent of death on the emaciated figure as he walked in front of them until he reached the black roan.

Iron Eyes paused, then ducked under the hitching rail and grabbed the bridle of the handsome horse. Some said the James brothers rode black roans like this one, but it was another equally dangerous outlaw whom the bounty hunter sought.

The sound of his sharp spurs rang out their deathly melody as the painfully lean figure moved alongside the roan until he reached the saddle-bags.

He squinted. The flickering lantern light graced the tan-coloured leather of the nearest satchel. The large black letters B.J.M. were burned into the satchel flap.

Iron Eyes shook his head as if in confusion at the owner of the bag's stupidity or arrogance. Why would any man with a bounty of $5,000 on his head have his initials branded into his saddle-bags?

'Buffalo's either confident that no right-minded critter will draw down on him or he's just plumb loco,' Iron Eyes muttered. He ran a hand along the rump of the sturdy animal before noting, 'No lather. That means this horse has been here a while.'

Iron Eyes emerged from the line of horses and stopped. This end of town was virtually shut down for the night, he thought. His head tilted. His long hair fell before his deadly eyes as he studied the rest of the wide street.

Beyond the stagecoach it seemed as if every other building was lit up for business. His knowing eyes reasoned that somewhere among them must be where the outlaw and his cronies were.

His spurs jangled as he continued back to his waiting mount and pulled the reins free of the pole. He was thoughtful as he grabbed the saddle horn and raised his boot to step into the stirrup.

In one fluid action Iron Eyes eased himself up on to the high-shouldered palomino and gathered in his reins before turning the animal away from the other horses.

Throughout the entire action the notorious hunter of men had not taken his eyes away from the array of saloons and gambling halls.

'Buffalo must be in one of them damn buildings down yonder, horse,' he reasoned, jabbing his spurs hard into the stallion to get it moving again. 'He's either drinking or eating or gambling or just planning on something. His kind never waste time in little towns like this'un unless they got something in mind.'

The palomino trotted as once more the bullet-coloured eyes of its master studied each of the buildings even more carefully than he had done previously. Iron Eyes had heard a lot of tales about the deadly McCoy. He had heard that when the outlaw had robbed a bank or held up a train he somehow disappeared. There would never be any sign of him until he appeared again to strike at a new target.

As the horse drew closer to the stagecoach a dozen theories flashed through the mind of the bounty hunter. He recalled a time three years earlier when he had cornered one of Buffalo Jim McCoy's men called Hal Taggart. Before Taggart had died he had hinted that after McCoy had executed a daring act of bank-robbing or the like he would take his ill-gotten gains to San Francisco. There he would live in luxury until he required additional funds. Only then would Buffalo Jim return to the Wild West and recruit a new gang.

It made sense to Iron Eyes.

The folks of San Francisco were well known never to enquire where anyone's wealth originated.

He hauled back on his reins and stopped the stallion.

Sally glanced down at the horseman.

'Was it his horse?' she asked.

'I reckon so, Squirrel. I figure it is,' Iron Eyes drawled and then released the hammer of his gun before poking it next to its twin in his belt.

She rubbed her mouth on the back of her shirt-sleeve. 'I thought we was just coming here for provisions, Iron Eyes. How come you're all fired up about this varmint?'

'I ain't fired up,' he protested. 'I just don't like knowing there's a valuable bounty someplace near. If he spots me before I see him we could be drawing bullets like flies to an outhouse, that's all.'

'I'm thirsty.' Sally grabbed her Winchester from out of the box and cranked its lever. A spent casing flew over her shoulder as she frowned at him. 'I'm also damn hungry. I could eat a whole mess of grub right about now.'

Iron Eyes inhaled deeply and looked around. 'There's a café across the street, Squirrel. Why don't you head on over there and get them to rustle us up some vittles and I'll head on into one of these saloons and buy us some whiskey?'

'What about the team?' Sally pointed at the team of six horses. 'We ought to have them watered and grained for the night.'

'We will,' Iron Eyes growled and jabbed a finger at the air. 'There's a damn livery at the far end of the street, gal. We'll take them there after you've eaten and I've bought us some whiskey.'

She nodded and smiled. 'Sounds like a plan.'

The bounty hunter watched as the

feisty female climbed down to the sand with her trusty carbine clutched in her left hand. He then started to pat his pockets.

'What you looking for, beloved?' she asked coyly as she walked to the door of the stagecoach and opened it. 'You're out of cigars.'

Iron Eyes glanced at her as she hauled her canvas travelling bag out of the interior of the coach and then slammed the door.

'I thought I had me a few golden eagles,' he muttered. 'I was gonna give you one to pay for the grub.'

She brushed by the stallion and started to walk barefoot towards the café. 'You had ten golden eagles, Iron Eyes.'

The horseman allowed his palomino to walk a few steps behind the youngster. 'What do you mean, that I *had* ten gold eagles, Squirrel gal?'

She looked over her shoulder and smiled. Even the layers of trail dust could not hide her natural beauty. Not even from the eyes of the deadly bounty hunter.

'I got them now,' she announced, raising the canvas bag. 'I got them in here.'

Iron Eyes' expression changed to one of total bewilderment as he watched her step on to the boardwalk outside the well-illuminated café.

'You robbed me, Squirrel?'

She paused, lowered her chin and looked through her unkempt golden fringe.

'It ain't possible for a wife to steal from her beloved husband, darling. I just took them for safe keeping when you was getting some shut-eye.'

He steadied his mount.

'Hold on a minute,' Iron Eyes fumed. 'I had them coins in my pants pockets. You bin poking them little hands of yours into my pants pockets again?'

She smiled up at him and fluttered her long lashes. 'I surely did. Guess what? I found out why you don't like me sliding my fingers in there.'

Iron Eyes looked sheepish. 'What you mean?'

'You've got something else in there and it sure got a mind of its own.' Sally roared with laughter. 'Damn thing almost bit my fingers off.'

The embarrassed horseman allowed his mount to back away from the small female. He watched her enter the café. The aromatic aroma of good cooking filled his nostrils but he had another appetite that he needed to satisfy first. He had not tasted even the cheapest whiskey in nearly three days and that was one thing Iron Eyes intended to rectify before he did anything else.

He swung the tall animal around and was about to spur towards the closest of the town's abundance of saloons when her words hit him.

He looked briefly over his wide shoulder and shouted at the top of his voice. 'Hold on there. We ain't married, Squirrel. Hell, I'd recall that kinda tragedy. We ain't even betrothed by my reckoning.'

Iron Eyes jabbed his spurs hard and guided the stallion towards the saloon. He looked up and read the name that was painted proudly on its wooden façade above the porch.

The Longhorn Saloon.

2

The four outlaws trailed Buffalo Jim McCoy like obedient hounds along the boardwalk. It had been a long walk from where they had left their five mounts to reach this section of Lobo but that was the way McCoy worked. He would not give the order for their horses to be moved until shortly before he intended to strike. The outlaw glanced at the stone edifice and then rubbed his chin. A smile crossed his face.

Denver Short paused at McCoy's shoulder. He placed a cigar between his lips and then struck a match. The smoke drifted on the night air as the gang observed the massive bank.

'Are you sure this'll work, Buffalo?' Short asked.

The younger, more fearful members of the gang looked nervously at both men. They had never seen the notorious McCoy questioned before, but they had seen him kill.

'I'm sure OK, Denver,' McCoy replied. He rested his gloved hands on the grips of his holstered weapons, and turned to face the others. 'Look at that bank, boys. One day when you're old and grey you'll be bragging how you were the first outlaws to break into that monster.'

The outlaws were laughing in unison when a shadow was cast across their paths. McCoy spotted it first and swung on his heels to face the creator of the shadow.

The man was heavily set. He looked as if he had been carved from the same stone as the bank they were observing. He moved towards them.

'Howdy, Buffalo,' he hissed. 'It must be the longest while since we bumped into one another.'

McCoy stood ahead of his four men. His eyes studied the form and then focused on the bearded face. He knew this character well, but it was a knowledge he wished he did not possess.

'If it ain't Artie Davis,' he observed.

Davis walked closer to the five men. He was a big man by any yardstick. Taller and wider than most. His gut hung over his belt buckle.

'I got to ask myself, what would Buffalo McCoy be doing in a little town like Lobo?' Davis posed the question as he reached McCoy. 'Could it be that the famous Buffalo Jim has heard about the silver mine payroll?'

McCoy smiled up at the far larger man. It was like talking to a haystack.

'It might be.'

The calculating Davis clasped his hands together and rubbed them in expectant glee. 'And you wouldn't mind cutting me in, would you? For old times' sake. After all, you owe me.'

Buffalo Jim McCoy had grown no friendlier but a lot wiser in his years away from the West. Some said that each time he returned to his old hunting grounds he was even more ruthless.

'I owe you?' McCoy asked drily.

'You surely do, Buffalo,' Davis replied with a firm nod. 'You owe me and you're gonna pay me an equal share or I'll go wake up this town's sheriff. Reckon he'd be mighty interested in learning that Lobo got itself a gang of thieves in its midst.'

The four other outlaws remained observers. They kept out of the way of their leader as McCoy strayed away from the bunch. Davis followed his former boss to the edge of a corner and rested a massive hand on McCoy's shoulder. He tried to intimidate the smaller man but failed.

'I figured this deal would draw you out of the woodwork, Buffalo.' Davis laughed triumphantly. 'I just had me the feeling that you couldn't resist a silver mine payroll. I rode here on the off-chance that you'd show. You did just like I figured you would.'

'You're pretty damn smart, Artie.'

McCoy brooded as he stepped down on to the dusty ground and wandered into the black shadows of the gap between two buildings. With each step McCoy took he could hear the larger man laughing as he kept pace with the deadly outlaw. 'Too smart for your own good.'

Artie Davis placed a hand on the shoulder of the man and swung him around.

'Hold up there, Buffalo. What we gonna do?' Davis asked.

'You don't have to do nothing at all, Artie,' Buffalo Jim McCoy said in a rasping whisper. 'You ain't gonna do nothing except die.'

The words had only just sunk into the brain of the larger man when he felt a fist punch him hard and low. At first the massive Davis just grinned at the pathetic punch.

Then he realized that the clenched fist had held a weapon.

His eyes glanced down and stared in disbelief at the blood that spread out over his large chest and belly. His hands went to grab hold of McCoy's throat when his eyes widened at the sight.

Even the darkness of the shadows could not hide the fearsome truth from the large Davis. His eyes stared down at the blade of the knife in McCoy's hand. Its fine-honed edge dripped with gore. Then he felt it being thrust into him again and again. Each strike took more and more of the huge Davis's life from him.

'You stinking rat.' Davis staggered forward and then fell on to his face. McCoy knelt and slid the blade across the throat of the fallen man. It was all over in seconds.

The four outlaws had watched it all with open mouths. None of them dared utter a word.

They stood silently watching their leader as he covered the body in garbage until it was hidden from view.

As though nothing had happened, Buffalo Jim McCoy led them away from the carnage and cut a path to a hardware store. Then, after emerging again into the dimly lit street, he started back into the very heart of Lobo. The outlaws moved from the lantern light into the darkest part of the street. Buffalo Jim stopped in the very middle of the wide thoroughfare and raised a hand to halt his followers.

Something had caught Buffalo Jim's eye. It was something which he had not expected to see. The tall outlaw lowered his head until his chin rested on the knot of his bandanna as he wiped the blade clean and slid it into his belt. He said nothing as he watched the haunting figure 200 yards away.

Denver Short moved to his paymaster's shoulder. Cigar smoke drifted from his lips.

'What you seen, Buffalo?' he asked as Bob Vagas, Tom Brown and Stacy Doyle stopped next to their two cohorts.

McCoy rested his knuckles on his gun grips and started to shake his head in disbelief at what his eyes were seeing.

'Iron Eyes!'

The four men squinted hard at the distant horseman astride the powerful palomino stallion. Doyle ventured close to Short and McCoy.

'I know the name but I figured he was just some kinda tall story, Buffalo. Are you sure that's him?' Doyle wondered.

'He's tall OK but he ain't no damn story, Stacy,' Buffalo Jim said grimly. 'That's the most dangerous bastard I ever met and I've sure met a heap of bastards in my time.'

Short exhaled smoke. 'Why don't you handle him the same way as you did with big Artie?'

'Iron Eyes don't know how to die.' McCoy's voice trembled as he spoke.

'Quit fretting, boss. He's just one man,' Brown ventured innocently. 'There's five of us and no one critter can take on them odds and survive.'

'He can.' McCoy shook his head again. 'I've seen him take on more men than you've had soiled doves, Tom. Heed my words. That critter is trouble.'

'You mean them stories about him are true?' Vagas asked, stroking his holstered gun. 'He is that dangerous?'

Buffalo Jim walked on again until they reached the front of a shuttered store. The porch roof kept the starlight from them. Again the leader of the gang rested. He placed a hand on the wooden upright and continued to glare at the horseman.

'That critter killed my top gunhand,' he recalled. 'I never seen such shooting. Iron Eyes was shot to ribbons and he still killed my best hand. He ain't human.'

'He was the one who killed Taggart?' Doyle asked.

'Yep.' Buffalo nodded. 'He also killed every one of my best gang and pocketed the bounty on their heads. I only escaped by leaping into a raging river. He must have figured I was drowned 'coz he didn't follow. That man ain't just dangerous, he ain't human.'

'What we gonna do?' Brown wondered. 'Are we gonna call off the job until he heads on out of town, Buffalo?'

Buffalo Jim McCoy brooded. He knew what he should do in order to stay clear of such a creature but he was on a deadline and if he were to wait, all would be lost.

'We can't call off this job.' McCoy looked across the street to the proudest of all the buildings in the town of Lobo. His eyes narrowed as they focused on the four-letter word carved into its stone façade. 'We have to rob that bank tonight. We ain't got no alternative, boys. Not unless we wanna ride away from here with empty pockets, that is. That bank has the payroll for all of the territory's silver miners in its safe. Tomorrow they'll pay that money out to all of the mine agents and it'll be gone. This job has to done tonight or we're gonna come up mighty short on our expectations. We have to rob it tonight or not at all.'

The four men surrounding McCoy gave out a long, collective sigh. Doyle stared at the box of ammunition he had just purchased in the hardware store.

'You reckon we got a chance of getting out of this town after we rob the bank, Buffalo?' Doyle asked. 'I mean, with that damn critter in Lobo.'

'I heard he was a dead man who can't be killed,' Vagas said nervously.

'I heard that as well,' Brown stammered.

'He's alive OK,' McCoy contradicted his new recruits. 'I've seen him bleed. Ghosts can't bleed. He's just bin lucky until now.'

'Let's hope his luck runs out real soon,' Short said, and snorted.

Buffalo Jim nodded. 'All we gotta do is stay out of his way for a few hours. Even Iron Eyes has to sleep sometime. We just wait until he's bedded down for the night and then we mosey on over to the bank.'

It was a nervous Bob Vagas who bit his lip. 'We oughta be safe if'n we just find us a place to play some stud poker for a while.'

McCoy gritted his teeth and shook his head.

'Nope, I got me a better idea. We'll find us some real soft ladies to entertain us. Iron Eyes never bothers with womenfolk,' he told them as he recalled with a smile. 'They make him real nervous. By my reckoning the safest place in all of Lobo will be a whorehouse.'

Short inhaled deeply on his cigar and gave a knowing smile at the rest of the gang.

'Hell, Buffalo. I'm willing to waste a couple of hours in the arms of friendly females,' he announced.

'Me too.' Doyle laughed.

'C'mon, boys. Follow me.' McCoy turned and led his four hand-picked outlaws back into the shadows towards the nearest glowing red lantern.

The outlaws followed.

3

The gaunt figure dismounted, looped his reins around the hitching rail and stepped up on to the boardwalk outside the Longhorn. Iron Eyes walked to the end of the boardwalk and stared around the dark street. Every fibre of his lean frame warned him that Buffalo Jim was near by but no matter how hard he stared, he could not see the famed outlaw. A large man built mainly of muscle moved close to the bounty hunter. In a flash Iron Eyes had stepped before the man. Their eyes burned into one another for a few moments.

'What in tarnation do you want?' the burly man asked. A giant finger jabbed into the bounty hunter's bony chest.

There was a chilling silence as Iron Eyes just brushed the stabbing digit's imprint away. He gritted his small sharp teeth and slowly muttered.

'Your cigar.'

The large man gave out a grunting laugh. He shook his head and then snorted.

'Buy your own.'

Iron Eyes gave a twisted grin. It had all of the hallmarks of a man who was not amused or intimidated. The larger man went to move around the obstacle but the bounty hunter anticipated the action. Again the bounty hunter blocked the larger man's progress.

'Listen up,' the man growled angrily. 'You don't know who I am, do you?'

'I reckon you don't know who I am either,' Iron Eyes replied. 'If you did you'd surely hand me that smoke.'

The massive man leaned towards the bounty hunter. 'Who in tarnation are you?'

'My name's Iron Eyes.'

'What kinda dumb name is that?' The man was still unimpressed. He raised a hand to push the thinner man aside. That was a mistake. The sound of the arm being snapped filled the air. Then as the man was about to scream out in agony, Iron Eyes head-butted him into unconsciousness. The man crashed into the boards like a felled tree. Iron Eyes reached down, plucked the cigar from the man's mouth and gripped it with his own teeth.

'Much obliged, friend,' he said through a cloud of smoke and he stepped over the prostrate figure. 'Nice to do business with you.'

A hundred thoughts drifted through his mind as he stood like an ominous phantom beside the porch upright. There were a few other people moving through the glimmering lantern light but none of them posed any problems. Iron Eyes ran his hand along his neck and then turned. Squirrel Sally's six-horse team stood chafing the ground with their hoofs but the bounty hunter had another thought nagging at him.

He was thirsty.

He paced back along the boards. His spurs rang out as the tall, skeletal figure placed a bony hand upon the top of the swing doors. His eyes screwed up and surveyed the people within the saloon.

Smoke encircled his head as he studied them. He puffed on the last of the cigar's flavour.

Iron Eyes rubbed his throat. He was still thirsty and that was all that concerned him. Then he recalled that Squirrel Sally had taken all his loose coins with her into the café opposite. Iron Eyes fumed for a few moments, then recalled something. His thin fingers peeled back his bloodstained shirt pocket and finally located a fifty-dollar bill. He carefully unfolded the blood-stained banknote and pushed it into his pants pocket.

'That should be enough.' He pushed the swing doors inward and entered.

The bounty hunter heard the sound of the tinny piano which came from the depths of the Longhorn. He took a few strides and the saloon fell silent.

His hands were ready for action. Iron Eyes flexed his fingers as he walked through the thick clouds of cigar smoke and made his way towards the counter of the bar.

With each stride Iron Eyes had seen each and every one of the faces within the Longhorn. None gave him cause for concern so he continued on towards the long bar counter.

He had not recognized any of their faces.

None of them were wanted.

As the tall, gaunt figure reached the bar he noticed that the men turned away in a mixture of fear and revulsion. The bargirls knew that it was their job to greet strangers but not even the most skilled of them could move a muscle. They had all seen many things in their time but nothing had prepared them for the sight of Iron Eyes.

This was no man, they silently told themselves.

To all intents and purposes this was a creature cast in the bowels of Hell by the Devil himself. He barely looked human.

His face bore evidence of every fight and battle he had waged over the years. He was a living corpse and yet something inside him refused to quit.

The people within the saloon moved away as Iron Eyes reached the bar. They could not look at this atrocity for any length of time. This was no true living man but a mistake who had yet to return to the fiery place which must have spawned him.

The barman stood his ground.

He summoned some depth of courage and exhaled as the creature moved closer and closer to the bar counter.

'What do you want?' the bartender asked.

The strange figure glanced from behind his veil of long limp hair and then straightened up to his full impressive height. A concerted gasp travelled round the bar as though by magic. He plucked the last of the cigar from his lips and then dropped it.

His boot crushed it into the sawdust.

Iron Eyes placed both his hands

upon the bar counter's damp surface. For a few moments he did not speak. He calculated the situation like a moneylender working out his profit.

The bartender licked his dry lips and ventured forward.

'I asked you a question,' he croaked. 'What'll it be?'

'Whiskey,' Iron Eyes said in a quiet, rasping way. 'Give me a dozen bottles and rustle up some cigars.'

The bartender laughed, then placed his hand on the counter. His eyes narrowed as he studied the horrific features. Iron Eyes did not look as though he had two cents to rub together.

'You got any money, handsome?' he joked. 'This ain't no charity I'm running here. Hard cash for hard liquor.'

The question burned into the tall stranger.

Iron Eyes gave a slow nod. 'Sure I got me money.'

The bartender was feeling confident

and well protected by the wide counter between them. He started to polish glasses before his newest and most ugly of customers. It was as if he were mocking the stranger.

'You say that you've got money but my boss don't pay me to be blind when it comes to cash,' the bartender continued. 'How do I know that you just ain't joshing with me? Show me your money or the whiskey stays exactly where it is.'

Again there was a long silence.

Iron Eyes gave a series of slow nods. He was fuming but decided to allow the mockery to continue. He lowered his head until his face was no longer visible.

'I've got the money,' Iron Eyes repeated. 'I'd be obliged if'n you'd get me the whiskey and the cigars.'

The bartender glanced at the others on both sides of him as though he were sharing a joke with them. He laughed and then took one too many risks. He leaned close to the stooped head. That was his first and final mistake.

'Fella? I don't reckon you can rustle up spit.' The words burned like a branding-iron into the very soul of the emaciated figure. 'Now head on out and don't be bothering me again. Savvy?'

Faster than any of the patrons had ever seen anyone react before, Iron Eyes struck like a sidewinder. His hands left the counter and grabbed the bartender's head violently. The skeletal fingers clawed at the neck of the bartender. Then, whilst one hand held it in check the other snatched a Navy Colt from his belt.

The gun barrel hit the bartender between his eyes.

The cold steel pressed into the temple of the terrified bartender. All the helpless bartender could now do was listen to the words of the man who at any moment might blow his brains all over the saloon.

The shocked patrons of the saloon moved back in stunned awe. They all expected the same thing and that was a noisy, bloody end to the situation.

'I'm gonna say this just one more time, barkeep,' Iron Eyes growled into the ear of the bartender. 'Get me the whiskey or I'll surely kill you. Do you understand me?'

The bartender gave out a whimper.

Iron Eyes tilted his head. One of his eyes glared through the strands of limp hair at the face of the terrified man.

'Do you savvy?'

The man blinked his reply.

The bartender stood shaking as the bounty hunter released his vicelike grip and aimed his gun straight at him. For a few moments the bartender thought that his end was nigh. He closed his eyes and awaited the last noise he expected to hear. It would be the sound of the gun being fired.

'Well? What are you waiting for?' Iron Eyes slammed his gun on the counter. 'Do what I done told you.'

'A dozen bottles?' the bartender asked.

'Damn right,' Iron Eyes hissed.

As the trembling bartender scooped up every bottle of whiskey from under the counter and placed them next to the silent bounty hunter, Iron Eyes dropped his six-shooter inside the bullet-filled pocket.

There was a long silence as the bartender hovered like a horsefly around the tail of a pony. He was shaking and yet he still managed to clear his throat.

'Ah, hem.'

The bounty hunter lowered his head again and stared straight at the man.

'Now what do you want?'

'I sure hate to ask but you do intend paying me for these. Right?' the bartender stammered nervously as he set the last of the dozen bottles on the counter.

Iron Eyes gave a twisted smile. 'Not until you bring me the cigars, friend. Not until you bring me the cigars.'

The box of cigars had no sooner been placed on the counter beside the twelve bottles of whiskey than the swing doors were flung open.

Once again, faster than any of the people inside the Longhorn had ever seen anyone move before, Iron Eyes turned, drew and cocked both his Navy Colts.

The sheriff stood frozen to the sawdust beneath his boot leather. The lawman raised his hands and stared at the deathly figure crouched before him. A man who had two Navy Colts trained upon him.

'What the hell are you?' he asked.

The lethal bounty hunter straightened up and released the hammers on his weaponry before poking them into his belt. He strode up to the man with the tin star pinned to his vest and observed him carefully. He then spoke.

'My name is Iron Eyes.'

4

The lawman watched as the emaciated figure placed the last of the whiskey bottles in the driver's box and then turned away from the stagecoach. He had never before seen anyone who looked quite so dead before but knew that this man was far more dangerous than any other stranger who had previously visited Lobo. Iron Eyes had heard most of the lectures men with tin stars tended to use but his guts were aching and he wanted to join Squirrel Sally over in the café. He would allow the sheriff his moment of glory and then ignore the fat old man and do exactly what he liked.

Sheriff Lomax White had never seen anything quite like the strange creature in front of him but he had seen Navy Colts before and knew the kind of damage they could inflict. He had also heard of the name of Iron Eyes and knew what the man was capable of doing. White walked around the tall stranger as Iron Eyes lit one of the cigars he had just purchased.

His cold eyes studied the lawman intently.

'I don't want you to get me wrong but you strike me as being trouble, boy,' White said cautiously. 'Real big trouble and I don't like trouble in my town. Do you understand me, boy? Folks around here pay me to keep trouble away from them and until now I've done a real good job.'

'Reckon I understand you right enough.' Iron Eyes remained like a statue as he puffed on his cigar. Sheriff White continued to circle the bounty hunter.

'My problem is you, boy.'

Iron Eyes inhaled and watched the nervous lawman as he circled him.

'It is?'

'It surely is.' White pointed a finger at the bounty hunter but continued his pacing. 'I try to keep this town calm. I try and keep the town settled. There are a few fist fights here and there but on the whole Lobo is peaceful. Damn peaceful. You make folks nervous and nervous folks are unhappy folks.'

Iron Eyes nodded. 'Reckon they are.'

White stopped and pointed at Iron Eyes. 'I'm glad we understand one another. Trouble is, you showed up. I ain't got no bad feelings against even the ugliest of folks like yourself but you just kinda upset folks. Do you understand me, boy?'

Iron Eyes looked upward at the stars. 'What are you trying to say, Sheriff?' he asked.

'Simply this, boy.' White stepped close to the tall figure with the cigar in his mouth. 'Get out of Lobo. That'll make everyone happy again. Will you do that for me, boy?'

Iron Eyes rubbed his thumb along his lower lip, then plucked the cigar from his teeth. He tapped the ash from it and looked down on the lawman.

'I'll be leaving.'

White beamed. 'You will?'

'Sure. When I'm through here, I'll leave.' Iron Eyes dropped his cigar and watched as the night breeze blew the burning tip around the area. A dozen fireflies could not have made a fancier show.

Sheriff White raised an eyebrow. 'What does that mean exactly, boy?'

Iron Eyes looked straight into the face of the elderly sheriff and smiled. 'It means when I'm through I'll be heading out of this town.'

Lomax White grabbed one of the bony hands and shook it like a man pumping for water.

'That's fine, boy. As long as you keep on riding I'll be a mighty happy man.'

Iron Eyes swung around on his heels and stepped down from the boardwalk. He strolled across the wide empty street towards the café. With each step the sound of pockets filled with loose bullets filled the air.

The sheriff looked confused as he

chewed on the words of the deadly bounty hunter. He waved a hand.

'Hold on there just a damn minute, boy. Where the hell are you going? I thought you was gonna leave Lobo?'

Iron Eyes tilted his head and glanced back at the lawman through his mane of black hair. A cruel grin etched itself across his features. White was still standing beside the stagecoach with his arms flapping.

'I'm just headed to the café to have me some vittles.'

Sheriff White dragged his hat from his head, mopped his brow, then returned it. He stepped to the rim of the boardwalk.

'I thought we had an agreement, boy. You said you were going,' he shouted.

Iron Eyes stepped up on to the boardwalk opposite and took hold of the café's door handle. He turned it and paused. A shaft of lantern light streamed out across the sand towards the lawman.

'I'll go when my partner is ready,

Sheriff.' The bounty hunter then gave a salute and entered the café.

Sheriff White stomped his boot on the boards and paced around for a few moments as he tried to think. Finally he exhaled loudly and walked forlornly to the stagecoach. He stepped across to one of the stagecoach's wheels and clambered up the side of the vehicle until he reached the driver's box. Lomax White pulled one of the bottles free and eased its cork from its neck. He looked at it. Iron Eyes had already consumed half of the bottle's contents.

White ran the palm of his hand over the bottle's neck and took a long swallow of the fiery liquor. Sitting on the high driver's seat he began to repeat the words of the bounty hunter.

''I'll go when my partner is ready, Sheriff',' the lawman mumbled before the gravity of the words dawned on him. 'Partner? Damn it all! The bastard has a partner. Now there's two of the critters in my town.'

The lawman raised the bottle to his dry lips and started to drink even more. One deadly bounty hunter in Lobo was bad enough but two was unimaginable.

5

The red-glowing lantern outside the house was dim. It could barely be seen from the main street but those who frequented the establishment needed no introduction. Everyone in town knew where it was and what it was.

The five outlaws had visited many similar places in their time but on this occasion it was different. This time none of them had ventured from the ornate parlour to the rooms on the upper floor, much to the surprise and disappointment of the scantily dressed females.

They had other thoughts to ponder with.

Other more pressing things on their minds.

Buffalo Jim McCoy had situated himself close to one of the front windows, from where he could see the main street. It was not a good view but good enough for the cold and calculating mind of the gang's leader.

The street was narrow and quite short.

There was only one way to and from the house with the red light and that suited McCoy just fine. He wanted to be able to see if anyone entered the side street and approached the sweet-perfumed establishment.

So far not one single person had.

McCoy wondered if Iron Eyes was here in Lobo hunting his prey, or was the bounty hunter simply passing through? Whichever it was the outlaw did not like the nagging thought that at any moment he might blunder into them. For Iron Eyes was unlike other men. He did not know when to quit. There was no stepping back for that skeletal creature.

Iron Eyes had only one direction and that was forwards.

The ruthless outlaw glanced across the parlour at his four hired men. A normal man might have smiled but not McCoy. He watched his four well-armed cohorts being comforted by the ladies with cold understanding.

He had instructed each of them not to leave the room and so far his orders had been obeyed. Yet even Buffalo Jim McCoy was aware that there was only so much any man could stand before his resolve broke.

McCoy snapped his fingers.

Every eye in the parlour turned towards the man who sat near the window.

'Don't get too friendly with these whores, boys,' he snarled. 'We still got a job to do and a man with his sap diluted ain't worth a plug nickel. Understand me, boys?'

Each of the outlaws gave a resentful grunt.

'What time do you make it, Denver?' McCoy asked his top gun as he lit yet another cigar.

Denver Short pushed a half-naked female from his lap and rose to his feet. He adjusted his pants and paced across the room to his leader. He had his pocket watch open and was staring at the hands of the expensive timepiece.

'I got me eleven ten, Buffalo,' he answered.

'Still mighty early,' McCoy said before reaching for his glass and downing its amber contents. 'Too early for us to do anything.'

'What about the horses?' Short wondered.

Buffalo Jim nodded. 'Yeah, the horses. We should bring them up from the other end of town before we do anything else.'

A female moved up behind Short and started to run her small, powdered hands all over him. The outlaw ignored her advances.

'I could go and get the horses and bring them here, Buffalo,' he said.

'Good thinking, Denver.' McCoy nodded as he sucked on his smoke. 'Take Stacy with you and don't make it look too obvious what you're doing. Right?'

'Right, Buffalo.'

Denver Short peeled the female off him and moved across the parlour to the others. He pointed at Stacy Doyle.

'C'mon, Stacy,' Short said. 'We got a job to do.'

Reluctantly Doyle pulled a young female hand from his lap and stood up. He touched the brim of his Stetson and then trailed behind Short, out of the room. The sound of the door slamming filled the house.

Vagas and Brown looked from their chairs.

'Where'd they go?' Vagas asked.

'Yeah, where in tarnation did them two go, Buffalo?' Brown added.

McCoy's expression told the two outlaws all they needed to know. He returned his gaze to the window and watched as both his outlaws moved through the shadows, away from the whorehouse.

A far more mature female moved towards McCoy and refilled his glass. She looked as if she had once worked as hard as her string of young apprentices, but no longer. Now she had a far more important duty.

'Tell me something: are your boys ever going up them stairs, Buffalo?' she asked coyly as she cradled the crystal decanter. 'Seems like a waste to sample the goods but never actually taste them.'

Buffalo Jim smiled at her.

'My boys can taste them goods all they like on their own time, Madam Rose. Right now they're on my time.'

The mature female nodded and moved away.

Buffalo Jim McCoy looked back through the window. He just caught sight of Doyle and Short as they turned the corner into the main thoroughfare. A brooding thought continued to nag at the corners of the outlaw's mind. The one man who could put an end even to the best-laid plans was in town and that thought festered inside the outlaw.

'Iron Eyes,' he whispered through gritted teeth.

6

The bounty hunter had barely spoken a word to Squirrel Sally throughout the entire time they had spent in the café as he brooded upon the events in Lobo. Something was brewing in the small town, yet Iron Eyes did not have any idea what that was. He knew that Buffalo Jim McCoy was somewhere in the town, but where and why? Iron Eyes had hardly consumed any of his meal either, and that enraged the feisty young Sally. He had toyed with his steak and eggs like a child trying to find a way of hiding the contents of his plate by clever manipulation of the food upon it.

'I'm gonna whip you damn hard if you don't eat something, Iron Eyes,' Sally scolded him. 'You hear me?'

Iron Eyes glanced up as though awoken from a dream.

'What you say, Squirrel?'

'Eat something,' she pleaded. 'You ain't nothing more than a bag of bones. Eat something while you got the chance.'

Iron Eyes was deep in thought. He glanced around the café as if unaware of anything within its small premises.

'What you thinking about?' Sally pressed. 'What's eating at you?'

His eyes looked at her. 'Did you say something, gal?'

'I sure did.' She leaned across the small round table and sliced half his steak. She then transferred it to her own plate and started to eat it. 'We spend days out in the wilderness and when we get a chance to have us some fine vittles you just daydream. If you ain't gonna eat it I will.'

Iron Eyes pulled a cigar from his pocket and struck a match. He sucked in smoke and kept staring into thin air.

'Why would Buffalo Jim McCoy's horse be in this town, Squirrel?' he pondered. 'That question's bin gnawing at my craw since I seen it down yonder.'

She looked up from her plate. 'I knew it. You bin hankering to kill some varmint for days, ain't you?'

The bounty hunter shook his head.

'Nope. I just don't like having outlaws close and not knowing where they're at or aiming their damn guns, that's all.' Iron Eyes sighed and looked through the steamed-up window at the sheriff on top of Sally's stagecoach. He rubbed the steam from the window.

'What you looking at?' Sally asked, her mouth full of food. 'Have you seen some critter with bounty on his head?'

'I was just looking at the sheriff, gal,' Iron Eyes replied, pointing at the lawman seated upon the driver's seat of her stagecoach.

Sally looked to where her betrothed was pointing. Her face fell as she stared at the lawman.

'He's sitting on my stagecoach,' she raged. 'What's he doing sitting on my stagecoach?'

'Easy, gal,' Iron Eyes said through a

cloud of smoke. 'He might be a fat old man but he is the law and what better protection is there than having the law sitting on your goods?'

She smiled. 'That is kinda sweet.'

'Mind you, he wants us to leave town pronto,' Iron Eyes added.

Her expression changed. 'He wants what?'

'Well, to tell the truth he just wants me to leave.' Iron Eyes tapped the ash from his cigar on to the floor. 'I reckon you could stay. Get a hotel room. Have a bath.'

The small female stood, irate, tore the napkin from her neck and plucked her Winchester off the table. She cranked the rifle's mechanism. A spent casing flew across the café towards the cook.

'If that sidewinding lawman thinks I'm gonna let him kick my betrothed out of town he's got another think coming.' She swung round and marched out into the night air. 'Bring my bag.'

Iron Eyes stood, lifted her bag and

walked after the furious female out into the street. He had lit her fuse and she was a stick of dynamite ready to explode.

The bounty hunter had heard all kinds of colourful language in his time, but nothing quite as colourful as the words that flowed from the mouth of Sally.

'Get off my damn stage, you fat old bastard,' Sally yelled out at the top of her lungs as she trained the deadly rifle on the lawman.

Before White could answer a bullet exploded from the rifle's barrel and whizzed a few inches over his head.

Still clutching the bottle, the sheriff protested: 'I'm the sheriff, young missy. I could throw you in my jail and toss away the keys.'

Sally fired again. This time the bullet was closer. So close that it ripped the hat from the lawman's head.

'Are you loco?' White screamed out. 'You could have killed me.'

'I'll do worse than that.' Sally spat.

'Throwing my beloved out of town is call for a stinking skunk like you to end up on Boot Hill.'

During the commotion Doyle and Short reached the café and knew that it was wise to keep going before they were spotted by the eagle-eyed bounty hunter. Both outlaws lifted up their collars as they raced past by the eatery and continued on towards their horses.

Nobody saw either man pass by the café as they moved in the shadows.

Nobody apart from Iron Eyes.

Iron Eyes stood directly behind the short female as she raged at White. The bounty hunter's honed senses had told him that there were men of interest walking through the shadows. They were men who did not want to be seen, but they had been spotted.

With his head drooped his bullet-coloured eyes trailed them from behind the mane of limp black hair. He said nothing and did even less. If these men had bounty on them Iron Eyes did not know about it.

As Squirrel Sally continued to rage at the sheriff Iron Eyes stepped between them and dropped the hefty bag on to the ground.

'What you doing, Iron Eyes?' Sally asked.

He touched her lips with his fingers, then approached as the terrified lawman reached the ground. White was shaking and Iron Eyes knew why.

'Who is she?' the lawman asked.

'She's my partner,' Iron Eyes stated.

Sheriff Lomax White made sure the lean bounty hunter remained between himself and the female's smoking rifle. His eyes were wide and unblinking.

'She's gonna kill me, boy.'

Iron Eyes shook his head. 'I surely doubt it, Sheriff.'

'How can you be sure?' White trembled as Iron Eyes led him away from the stagecoach and the lethal rifle.

'To be honest I can't,' Iron Eyes said. He rested a hand on the lawman's shoulders. 'You got any new Wanted posters, Sheriff?'

'I sure have.' White handed the bottle of whiskey to the gaunt figure. 'Follow me, boy. I bet there are dozens of outlaws you're just itching to ride out of town. Am I right?'

'You could say that.' Iron Eyes followed the sheriff towards his bleak office. 'Sometimes outlaws are closer than you think.'

Squirrel Sally stood holding her smoking Winchester in her small hands, looking stunned. 'I ain't finished with that old bastard yet, Iron Eyes, damn it. Bring him back.'

Both men increased their pace towards the office. They entered the unlocked darkness as the lawman fumbled for a match.

The sheriff struck the match along his pants leg and lit the wick of his lamp. He turned its wheel until the office was filled with light, then he started to look through a pile of posters.

'We got paper on dozens of loathsome critters here, boy,' he said gleefully. 'Just the kind I bet you love killing. Take a look and help yourself. They'll make good reading when you leave town.'

The tall man flicked through the pile of posters at a pace that the sheriff had never seen anyone manage before. Then he peeled two notices from the bunch and studied them with an eagle eye.

'You like those two, huh?' White gestured. 'Take them with you. They'll sure make good reading on the trail when you're on your way.'

The cigar smoke hung around the bounty hunter's head like a noose. He nodded to himself and folded the two posters up. His bony hand pushed them down into his deep jacket pocket, amid the bullets.

'Just like I figured,' Iron Eyes said through clenched teeth. 'Buffalo ain't on his lonesome.'

Sheriff Lomax White followed the taller man back out into the street. Both men were heading back to where the stagecoach was waiting.

'Buffalo?' White queried. 'What the

hell are you talking about, Iron Eyes?'

The bounty hunter stopped walking. He lifted the bottle, drained it, then cast it aside.

'You ever heard of Buffalo Jim McCoy, Sheriff?' Iron Eyes asked. He inhaled on his cigar again.

White nodded slowly. 'The name is kinda familiar.'

'Buffalo is an outlaw, Sheriff,' Iron Eyes told him. 'I've had my sights on him a couple of times but after he does a job he just vanishes. For years I've wondered where he goes and then it dawned on me. He heads off to a big fancy city and lords it with their finery. When he needs more money he heads back and strikes again.'

The lawman raised his eyebrows. 'What you telling me about this Buffalo critter for?'

'Because he's in Lobo, friend,' Iron Eyes said. 'And he ain't alone. He's got himself a gang with him and in my book that means just one thing.'

The fearful lawman grabbed the arm

of the bounty hunter and their eyes met. There was terror in the sheriff's aged face.

'But why is he here in Lobo? We ain't got nothing in Lobo worth a damn.'

The bounty hunter studied his cigar and tapped its ash against the wall. He then turned and stared out into the cool dark street.

'You've got a bank in this town, ain't you?' Iron Eyes drawled. 'That's all Buffalo needs. Just a bank.'

The sheriff looked suddenly stricken as he remembered that for once the town's small bank would have an abundance of money in its safe.

'Oh, my God. The bank's full to bursting with the cash for the silver mine payroll,' the sheriff gasped. 'It was shipped in here by Wells Fargo a couple of days back.'

'I reckon that's it, then. Somehow Buffalo got to hear about the payroll.' Iron Eyes sucked on the last of his cigar's smoke, then dropped the stinking weed and crushed it beneath his boot. A wry smile etched his crippled features as he stepped back towards the wide-open doorway.

'Hold on there, boy,' White stammered. 'You can't just tell me something like that and then walk away.'

The words of the veteran lawman stopped the bounty hunter in his tracks. Iron Eyes rubbed his gaunt face with his bony fingers.

'Why not, Sheriff?' he asked coldly.

'Because it just ain't right, that's why not,' White protested. 'I don't know what to do against a gang of seasoned outlaws. I ain't even got a deputy to help me, boy.'

Iron Eyes paused for a few moments. His eyes flashed around the silent street in search of the elusive prey he knew was close enough to spit at. Where was Buffalo Jim? he asked himself silently. Where was the elusive and very dangerous Buffalo?

He tilted his head. His icy glare burned into the old lawman. His busted eyebrow rose.

'You still want me to leave town, Sheriff?' Iron Eyes did not bother to listen to the answer to his question as he continued to stroll out into the shadows of the main street.

He already knew what that answer would be.

7

Iron Eyes glanced at the sturdy, stone-built bank and tapped his spurs even harder. He knew that nothing would happen whilst he was still in town. He also realized that Buffalo would never willingly show his hand until there was no other option. The bounty hunter had taken the young Sally's stagecoach to the livery stable so that the team of six horses could be watered and fed for the night. After that chore he had returned to the very centre of Lobo astride his palomino stallion. As the horse slowed its pace Iron Eyes felt sure that Buffalo was having his every movement watched by his cohorts.

The bounty hunter was certain that they would keep watching him until he left the small settlement. Only his departure would give Buffalo the confidence to believe that he could strike at the bank with impunity.

The sound of his horse's hoofs echoed off the wooden buildings spread out along the street as the grim-faced bounty hunter eased back on his reins. Iron Eyes reached the hotel and then slowly dismounted.

He looped his leg over the neck of his prized mount and slid to the ground. The haunting noise of his jagged spurs rang out but there seemed to be no one to hear it. Every saloon and store in Lobo had closed for the night. It was as if everyone somehow knew what was about to occur within the confines of the town.

Iron Eyes could feel the eyes of his enemies burning through the shadows into his flesh with each step he took. But Buffalo was smart and would not tackle the emaciated bounty hunter again if he could avoid it.

Iron Eyes led the palomino towards the hitching rail, tied a knot in the long leathers, then straightened himself up.

His eyes darted from one black shadow to the next as he stepped up on to the hotel boardwalk. Yet he did not see one living creature.

It was a thoughtful Iron Eyes who entered the hotel.

Somehow, an hour earlier, he had persuaded Sally to take a room and await his return from the livery, but as he strode into the well-illuminated lobby Iron Eyes realized that she would also have to be fooled in the same way as he intended to try and fool the outlaws who were observing his every move.

That was not going to be easy, he told himself.

Squirrel Sally was far harder to persuade about anything than any mere outlaw, and the long-legged bounty hunter knew it. Iron Eyes wondered how he was going to achieve that goal as he ascended the staircase two steps at a time. Sally was smarter than most and she knew it. He reached the landing of the small hotel and sighed.

The ruthless bounty hunter would willingly take on a dozen armed men in a shoot-out rather than argue with the feisty youngster.

Sally was the one creature he had encountered on his travels who always had an answer to whatever question he posed. She troubled Iron Eyes.

Iron Eyes paused and looked around the small landing. He had spent months vainly trying to shake the handsome young female loose but now, as he planned to leave the town without her, Iron Eyes felt strangely sad.

Logic told him that he would be returning, but he still harboured doubts. Not everything went to plan and he had the scars to prove it.

He paced down the dimly lit corridor towards the room he had rented for them. He stared at the door and the faded number upon its flaking surface. Room two was said to be the best in the small hotel, but considering that the entire building only had three rooms for hire that did not mean very much.

His hand rose. He knocked three times but did not get a reply. Iron Eyes became troubled. A hundred thoughts flashed through his mind as one hand took hold of the handle whilst the other pulled one of his trusty Navy Colts from his belt.

He turned the door handle at the same moment as he cocked the gun's hammer.

Iron Eyes entered swiftly yet silently.

The painfully thin man stood like a ghost with his cocked weapon held at arm's length. But all of his concerns had been ill-founded. His bullet-coloured eyes darted from behind the limp locks of his long hair. Every corner of the room was searched by his cold eyes.

Slowly the bounty hunter relaxed and lowered his gun hand.

He stared at the young, sleeping female like a man who had never witnessed such beauty before. The sight of Squirrel Sally sleeping upon the bed disarmed Iron Eyes completely. His eyes caressed her naked body the way most men's hands might have done. Iron Eyes hovered just inside the doorway like a vulture surveying its prey.

A desire such as he had never experienced taunted him. A bead of sweat traced down from his hairline and navigated the scarred features of his face.

Like a puma he walked silently across the room to the double bed and stared down at her petite form. She had bathed and looked oddly different to his seasoned eyes. He slid the deadly gun back behind his belt buckle, then paused.

She appeared so delicate.

He had never noticed that about her before. Her tough words and determined courage had blinded him to what she truly was.

Sally was nothing more than a young girl. A beautiful young girl. He inhaled as his heart pounded inside his tortured chest. The scent of her hair filled his soul as his thin arm reached down, grabbed the blanket and carefully covered her modesty.

Iron Eyes closed his eyes for a few seconds, then he began to back away from her sleeping body. Each step made him feel as though he were fighting against chains. Chains that had somehow entrapped him without his even knowing it. Had this tiny female roped and branded him without him even being aware of it?

He turned to close the door. Iron Eyes paused for a few moments and fought with the unfamiliar emotion.

It was long enough for him to stare at her again. His heart pounded even harder and yet he did not know why. He was excited. Exactly the same way he became when he closed in on his prey, but Sally was not his prey.

He shook his head but his thoughts grew no clearer. Whatever he was feeling it was totally unknown to him. Iron Eyes had thought that he knew most things but he knew nothing about the feeling which now consumed him. The slumbering Sally had made him realize that.

He eased the door shut behind him and lowered his head.

Iron Eyes turned and slowly retraced his steps back to the top of the landing. It felt as though he were carrying some invisible burden upon his wide shoulders. One that only he knew existed. He glanced around the lobby below. A thin, balding man sat reading a newspaper behind a desk.

Iron Eyes descended.

With each step the sound of the bullets in his pockets rattled like a gambler's dice. He walked like a phantom back across the lobby out into the street and moved towards his horse.

He was shaking as though afraid.

It was another thing that troubled Iron Eyes.

A tangled web of confusion followed the lone bounty hunter down from the hotel back to where he had left his sturdy palomino. His thoughts grew no clearer no matter how far he travelled.

White was propped against the hitching rail close to the nose of his stallion. The older man looked up as Iron Eyes reached his waiting mount once more.

'Do you reckon that this is such a good plan, Iron Eyes?' the sheriff asked the gaunt bounty hunter.

Iron Eyes pulled the reins free of the pole.

'It better be. It's the only one I've got, old-timer,' he replied in a low whisper.

Sheriff White stood. He watched as the thin, emaciated man stepped into his stirrup and lifted up from the ground. Iron Eyes swung his right leg over the high cantle of the Mexican saddle and lowered himself down.

Iron Eyes had never looked so confused before.

'We might get our butts kicked, boy,' White warned the horseman.

'We might.' Iron Eyes gathered his reins together in his bony hands and turned the animal around. He looked along the wide street and sighed heavily. Iron Eyes produced a cigar as though by magic and then slid it into the corner of his mouth. For the first time in all of his days the bounty hunter felt utterly perplexed. He struck a match with his thumbnail and cupped its flame. Smoke surrounded the mane of black hair as Iron Eyes exhaled.

Sheriff White stared up at the hideous rider's face bathed in the amber illumination of the street lanterns. It was totally blank. Iron Eyes chewed on the cigar and puffed as he readied the stallion beneath him.

'What you thinking about, Iron Eyes, boy?' the lawman asked the solemn horseman. 'Is something troubling you?'

'Apart from getting shot?' The words drifted from his mouth like the smoke that surrounded them.

The wily old lawman could hear something different in the tone of the rasping voice. Something that made him study the face even harder.

'There's something else, ain't there boy?' White pressed the bounty hunter.

'Tell me. What's eating at you? What's wrong?'

There was a painfully long silence. Then the hideous face glanced down at the lawman again.

Iron Eyes thought about the sleeping Squirrel Sally up in the hotel room. Images of her filled his mind and would not cease no matter how hard he tried to chase them from his thoughts.

He allowed the powerful stallion to drag a hoof at the ground, then he released his tight grip.

'Nothing,' he lied.

The palomino thundered down the main street. The sound of its hoofs echoed off the wooden buildings as its master allowed the animal to find its own pace.

Buffalo Jim McCoy stepped from the shadows as both horse and rider thundered past him. The outlaw signalled to his gang. The other four men emerged from the darkest shadows and trailed the ruthless McCoy to the bank.

It had started.

8

Within minutes McCoy had entered the bank and was making his way towards the safe. Like all of its counterparts throughout the West, the safe was reputed to be foolproof. As always Buffalo Jim McCoy had worked out every detail of his elaborate plan long before he had arrived in Lobo. Within moments of espying his arch enemy ride out of the small town he had begun to execute his plan. There was a precision about everything that McCoy did. One by one the boxes were ticked off in the exact order that he had planned.

This was not merely a bank job. This was an operation no less delicate than anything scalpel-wielding surgeons back East could ever equal. Buffalo Jim McCoy knew every weakness of the bank building and would prove in a handful of minutes that no bank is truly impenetrable.

The sound of the muffled explosion barely escaped the two-feet-thick granite walls but its vibrations spread like a cancer just below the surface of the ground. A few moments later the skilled outlaw leader would be relieving the bank of its valuable miners' payroll.

A short time later the gang would be ready to leave Lobo with their fortune. Iron Eyes had only just reached the outskirts of the desolate town when something alerted him to the fact that McCoy and his henchman had already struck.

His honed hearing had heard the strange sound of expertly placed explosives. Iron Eyes knew that this was not the usual sound of an explosion that marked an ordinary gang's work, but a far more subtle noise.

It had seemed more like a distant thunderclap than anything else, but Iron Eyes knew there was not a storm cloud in sight.

He reined his stallion in.

Throwing himself from his saddle Iron Eyes knelt and pressed an ear to the arid terrain. He could feel the strange vibrations still rippling through the ground.

Every instinct inside his dishevelled body told the bounty hunter that Buffalo Jim had struck. No one else could have moved that quickly or so purposefully.

Iron Eyes rose to his full height and grabbed hold of his reins again. His cold eyes stared back at the town. It was quiet and unaware of what was happening, he thought.

He mounted urgently and hauled the palomino around. He rammed his spurs into the flanks of the powerful animal and thundered back towards Lobo.

This was not the way he had planned it.

This was different.

He had underestimated his adversary. Iron Eyes had thought that McCoy would be more cautious. He had imagined that the devilish outlaw would bide his time before he dared strike. The sheer speed of the outlaw's actions had taken Iron Eyes by surprise.

Buffalo Jim McCoy and his gang must have moved in on the bank only seconds after he had ridden past the big, stone-built edifice, Iron Eyes concluded.

He whipped the shoulders and tail of his mighty stallion and forged ahead towards the middle of the town. Iron Eyes had thought that he would have to wait for hours before they actually invaded the bank.

This was too fast, he told himself. *This was far too soon*.

Standing in his stirrups of the charging stallion he urged the animal with all of his might. Iron Eyes knew that he had to reach the bank before the outlaws made their escape.

Within seconds the bounty hunter reached the outskirts of Lobo and drove his charge on. Even through the narrow streets he did not slow his frantic pace.

He rode like a man possessed by the Devil himself.

Any witnesses might have assumed that the Devil was what they saw if they had been unfortunate enough to set eyes upon the horrific sight. Few men could have looked more terrifying than Iron Eyes in full pursuit of his goal.

The faster he rode the more he appeared to be like an avenging angel. His long, matted mane of black hair flapped on his broad shoulders like the wings of a bat.

His eyes narrowed against the night air. His teeth were gritted in an unholy snarl. This was a warrior in search of a battlefield. Iron Eyes was ready to kill or be killed. It made no difference to a man who did not fear death.

The wide-eyed stallion ate up the ground beneath its hoofs as its rider travelled like a steam train through the streets of Lobo towards the very centre of the town.

Nothing could stop Iron Eyes when he had the scent of his prey filling his flared nostrils. He was blindly fearless and determined to kill each and every one of them.

Their Wanted posters had proclaimed them wanted dead or alive, and that suited Iron Eyes just fine. He never saw any point in taking prisoners when the law itself had branded them as being fair game.

With each powerful stride of his stallion all other thoughts had been wiped clean from his mind.

There was only one thing burning inside him now. It burned his innards like a branding-iron. It was the simple goal of getting the five outlaws he had warned the sheriff about in his gun sights.

Nothing else mattered.

Nothing else meant anything to the intrepid horseman.

He was possessed. Iron Eyes dragged his reins hard to his left and instead of riding into the main street, he drove his powerful horse up a narrow alleyway between two buildings. The deafening noise of his stallion's hoofs echoed off their walls.

Iron Eyes was not stupid enough to ride straight into the guns of his enemies. He had tried that before against Buffalo Jim McCoy and still bore the scars that that mistake had earned him.

The alley stopped abruptly at the end of the two buildings but there was a sharp corner to his left. Iron Eyes dragged the head of the stallion violently to its left and spurred. He was now heading for the rear of the large bank building. Each alley was darker than the last. The starlight seemed unable to find the ground. Black shadows spread across the lanes and spilled out over an array of other wooden structures. The big, stone-built bank dominated the entire settlement yet the bounty hunter did not slow his progress.

He continued to whip the long ends of his leathers across the cream-coloured tail of his mount. The animal responded to its master's urgency.

Iron Eyes would use the alleyways' every twist and turn to try and fool the outlaws as to where he was going to strike from. He knew that Buffalo would suspect that he would show up at some time.

It was all a matter of surprise.

As the horseman reached the rear of the big stone building Iron Eyes could not see anyone. Had he imagined the strange shaking of the ground moments earlier? Several thoughts scattered themselves in the mind of the confused bounty hunter. Maybe one of the many silver mines that surrounded Lobo was firing dynamite off even at this ungodly hour. Maybe one of the silver miners themselves was celebrating early the fact that tomorrow was payday.

Iron Eyes hauled rein and held the stallion in check.

His determined eyes searched for any sign that the bank had been the target of the muffled sound he had heard. He could see nothing, but his flared nostrils detected the scent of gunpowder.

He cursed the fact that little of the stars' eerie light could even reach this place let alone cast its illumination upon it. A score of black shadows stretched out before the troubled horseman. Any one of them might be hiding the outlaws and their lethal guns.

With a skill that few men ever acquire Iron Eyes kept his palomino standing totally still. The exhausted animal snorted at the ground as its master tried to figure out where the men he was hunting might be.

There were too many shadows, he kept telling himself. Only an owl could see anything clearly in the shades of darkness that faced him. Iron Eyes was many things but he sure was no owl.

He decided to urge the horse to step forward. His spurs tapped the flesh of the stallion and forced the animal to walk forward for a few yards. Then, just as he was about to quit and return to the edge of town, his keen eyesight spotted a slight movement just ahead of him.

A thin sliver of light cut across the rear of the bank from a narrow gap in a doorframe at the rear of the bank.

At last, he thought silently.

Finally he had seen something.

His razor-sharp instincts had been correct. The bank was being robbed just as he had concluded when he had felt the ground shaking beneath him.

His dark eyes searched.

Slowly Iron Eyes drew one of his Navy Colts, then looped his leg over the neck of the walking horse. He pulled his pointed boot-toe from the left stirrup and slid to the ground. Like a ravenous beast he crouched as the horse came to a halt once more.

He squinted hard beneath the belly of the palomino and moved like a phantom into the gloom of the blackest of the shadows. Only a lethally accurate bullet could halt the progress of the long, skeletal figure now.

Iron Eyes continued to move towards

the place where he had caught a brief glimpse of someone moving away from the bank.

With each step it became obvious that whoever he had spotted a few heartbeats earlier was now gone. The outlaw had vanished into the vapours of blackness, but where were the others?

Where were the four other deadly outlaws?

The bounty hunter reached halfway along the alleyway beside the imposing bank in search of a black shadow where he might rest. He soon found one and entered it. Iron Eyes pressed his back up against a wall and stared like a venomous sidewinder in search of one of the outlaws to sink his fangs into.

Where was Buffalo Jim McCoy? The question screamed into his thoughts, but there had been no answers. He knew that he could have continued to trail the figure he had seen up towards Main Street but that would have allowed the others to get behind him.

Even Iron Eyes did not relish being

trapped between two factions of the cunning gang. He remained against the wall shrouded in the blackest of shadows.

Only his haunting, bullet-coloured eyes remained visible from the gloom of the dense shadows. Iron Eyes held his gun beside his pants leg. He was barely breathing as his eyes darted around the area again in search of a target to shoot at.

There were no movements in the alleyway. Not even vermin dared move along its length as the hunter of men remained perfectly still against the wall.

Not even a hint as to where any of his prey might be. He lowered his head and allowed his long black locks to drape before his face. He closed his eyes and listened intently.

He strained to hear.

All he needed was just one sound to tell him exactly where the outlaws were. Then he would strike.

The betrayal of a clumsy boot on a broken branch. The creaking of an unoiled door hinge. Anything. He screwed up his eyes and listened.

Yet no matter how hard he tried there seemed to be no one there. He threw his head backwards. His long hair hit the wall behind his head. He returned his attention to the impressive bank. It was the only building in Lobo that looked as though it might be sturdy enough to withstand a gust of wind.

He glanced at his horse as it wandered back down the alley and started to eat the leaves from overhanging tree branches.

For what felt like an eternity he saw nothing. He was about to move away from the wall and return to his mount when suddenly every one of his honed senses alerted him.

A light from a lantern beamed out into the alley. The side door of the bank had been opened and three men emerged, carrying large canvas bank bags.

Like a moth Iron Eyes was drawn from his hiding-place in the shadows towards the light. He walked unseen at a slow, deliberate pace. Hidden by the blackness he moved towards the light and the men who slipped through its brief illumination.

The outlaws moved swiftly.

They were headed back to the main thoroughfare. Iron Eyes imagined that was where they had left their mounts. His pace grew quicker.

Only the last of their number lingered long enough in the alleyway to notice the approach of the deadly bounty hunter behind them. As Buffalo Jim McCoy and Vagas carried their burden along the side of the alley towards Main Street Tom Brown swung around on his heels. He dropped his bag and then dragged his six-shooter from its holster.

Iron Eyes was nearly blinded by the white flashes as Brown's gun blasted in his direction. The sound was deafening in the narrow confines of the alley. It thundered around its tall target. The bounty hunter felt the tails of his long coat being lifted by the three bullets that came from Brown's weapon.

The shots were too close, Iron Eyes thought. He threw his thin, gaunt frame to the side and fanned his gun hammer in quick succession.

He watched the outlaw buckle and stagger backwards before falling into a crumpled heap close to the bank's slightly ajar door. A narrow beam of lantern light lit up the stunned expression on the outlaw's face as Iron Eyes walked towards him. Brown was not dead but blood was squirting from the bullet holes in his torso. Half-dead Brown stared up at the hideous creature who approached him. It was like facing the Devil himself.

The wounded outlaw raised his gun.

Iron Eyes paused. His cold stare watched as the outlaw's shaking hand tried vainly to aim his weapon.

Without a hint of emotion Iron Eyes mercilessly fanned his gun hammer. The alleyway lit up briefly as a massive hole in Brown's chest spewed crimson gore around the scene.

Iron Eyes continued his pursuit of the others.

The bounty hunter had taken only three steps when another shot came down the alleyway at him. A huge chunk of debris was ripped apart as the bullet narrowly missed Iron Eyes' head and caught the stone wall. The bounty hunter ducked into the shadows as even more deadly lead sought him out.

The side of the wall shattered as even more shots hammered into it. Dust showered over the crouched bounty hunter. Iron Eyes brushed himself down as he exchanged one gun for its twin. He cocked its hammer, rose to his feet and then charged forward.

With each long stride Iron Eyes fired his weapon.

He was angry now. He hurt and was chewing on dust.

The air was thick with the acrid taste of the smoke that billowed from the barrel of the hot weapon. Iron Eyes spat, and shook the spent shells from the hot chambers of his gun as he approached the end of the alley. He stopped and angrily glared at the street lanterns.

They were unkind to anyone who yearned for cover.

Iron Eyes' thin fingers found fresh bullets deep within his pockets and forced them into the gun. As he slid the fresh ammunition into the smoking chambers he continued to search the street for the rest of McCoy's gang.

'You're gonna pay for shooting at me, boys,' he growled.

Another volley of bullets came from the distant shadows across the wide street. Iron Eyes could feel their heat as he ducked and was forced backwards. He crouched beside the wall of the granite building as his hands continued feverishly to reload both his guns.

The scent of acrid gunsmoke filled his nostrils as he snapped the last of the Navy Colts shut. He rammed one gun into his pants belt and pulled back the other's hammer until it was fully cocked.

'Say your prayers, Buffalo,' he whispered.

His eyes scanned the area. He remained crouched as he watched for any hint as to where the outlaws were. Iron Eyes snarled angrily as he noted the street lanterns again.

There were too many of them.

They were making him the target. The bounty hunter vowed to end that before any of the remaining outlaws got lucky. He stepped forward and aimed.

He fanned the hammer of the gun in his hand.

Two of the lanterns across the street shattered into countless fragments. Iron Eyes then turned on his heels and fired another bullet upward. The glass globe on top of the tall pole outside the bank exploded, casting darkness to the edge of the building.

He then used the newly created shadow to dash across to a water trough. More lead followed the bounty hunter. His narrowed eyes saw the red-hot tapers emerge from the blackest of the shadows and speed in his direction.

He threw his painfully lean body to the ground just as the outlaw's lead carved holes into the trough. He had only just hit the ground when plumes of water rose like ornate fountains into the air before showering over him.

The bounty hunter scrambled on to his knees. He crouched behind the trough. He was drenched to the bone. Iron Eyes crawled along the wet sand until he reached the very end of the bullet-ridden trough. He tilted his head and caught a glimpse of a horse.

It was the black roan.

Iron Eyes rose up from his knees.

'Oh, no you don't, Buffalo.' Iron Eyes spat angrily at the sight of the horse. 'You ain't getting away from me again that easy.'

He cocked his Colt again and blasted it.

'Chew on that.'

The black stallion made a sickening noise. Iron Eyes watched as the mighty creature reared up and then came crashing down on to the sand. As the roan fell on to its knees and rolled over Iron Eyes caught sight of a man running away from the stricken animal. A bright flash signalled to Iron Eyes that the fleeing outlaw was firing. Within seconds the heat of the bullet tore through his jacket sleeve and creased the flesh on his arm. He gazed at the torn fabric. The tear in his trail coat was fringed with blood. He flexed his fingers and felt the warm blood running down the sleeve to his wrist.

He shook his hand like a man swatting a fly.

Iron Eyes snarled as pain tore through his lean frame. He fired two more times. The shots hit the dying horse but not the outlaw he believed to be Buffalo Jim McCoy.

'Damn it all,' Iron Eyes cursed angrily as he shook the hot casings from his smoking gun. 'That blasted horse got in the way. I hate horses.'

The furious bounty hunter propped

himself against the frame of the trough. He reloaded the gun and only then did he give any thought to his own wound. He pulled his jacket down and glanced at his arm. It was bleeding from the graze as Iron Eyes pulled his jacket back up to his neck.

'It'll keep,' he whispered.

Iron Eyes twisted his lean body and fired quickly, then ducked back. Suddenly the trough erupted again and more plumes of water jetted upwards as the outlaws' leader kept him pinned down.

Iron Eyes wondered how long he would be trapped behind the small wooden trough of water. Then he heard the unmistakable sound of horses' hoofs.

Fearing that the remaining wanted men were making a break for freedom Iron Eyes rose up with both his Navy Colts in his bony hands. He cocked and fired each of the weapons quickly as even more bullets tore through the darkness in search of his hide.

Just as he thought two riders were making a break he saw the two horses rear up. Their riders leapt from the saddles and ran for cover as both animals fell in the centre of the street.

The bounty hunter felt the bullets hitting his long trail coat. His lightweight frame was knocked off its feet. He stumbled and toppled on to the boardwalk of the bank, cracking his head.

The sound of distressed horses filled his dazed ears.

Using every scrap of his stunned strength he forced himself up on to his legs again and blasted the last of his guns' bullets at the sound of the horses. The sickening noise of wounded horses filled the smoke-filled street.

He turned sideways to the sound, dropped one gun into his deep coat pockets and began once again to reload the smoking six-shooter in his hand. The entire street was filled with shadows and gunsmoke. Neither the outlaws nor the bounty hunter could see one another.

9

Iron Eyes could feel bullets passing within inches of his thin body but refused to obey his survival instincts and duck for cover. He remained defiantly standing until his gun was reloaded.

His hand cocked its hammer.

His eyes cleared. Then he saw the results of his handiwork. Two of the outlaws' horses were on the ground, kicking dust into the air. The payroll bags were still secured to their saddle cantles.

Iron Eyes stepped on to the trough and jumped across its broken structure. He landed and ran to where the horses lay. One had been killed outright whilst the other kicked at the air in a vain struggle to outrun death itself.

As the emaciated bounty hunter moved close to the animal he pressed his gun barrel into its temple. He was about to put the horse out of its misery when it gave out an eerie noise and died.

A handful of shots came through the smoke and darkness at him. Before the bounty hunter could move he felt one of the bullets hit him in his shoulder. This was not like the graze that he still nursed. This was worse.

Wounded, Iron Eyes fell between the pair of dead horses. As his shoulders hit the dry ground a dozen more shots passed within inches of where he lay.

Angrily Iron Eyes rolled over and checked his shoulder. The bullet had gone straight through his meagre flesh, leaving just a neat hole.

Smoke trailed from the hideous wound.

Iron Eyes scrambled back to his knees and lay across the saddle. He fired his weapon back and watched as three of the outlaws ducked into an alleyway. Iron Eyes reloaded the gun as he considered the situation into which he had managed to become trapped.

His weary eyes had seen three of them through the gunsmoke. Three of them. He clenched his fist and slammed it down upon the saddle.

Where was the fourth outlaw?

A sudden dread filled the mind of the wounded bounty hunter. He did not mind facing armed men whom he could see but he did not like the idea of being back-shot by one of McCoy's gang. He glanced around the area. Wherever the fourth man was Iron Eyes could not detect him.

He had an idea. His bony fingers unhitched one of the saddle's cinch straps and dragged it free of the horse. He pulled the hefty saddle up and placed it on the side of the body of the slain horse. He tied the cinch straps together, making a perfect loop.

Iron Eyes staggered back to his feet.

He hoisted the saddle up into the air and held it before his thin frame. He then slid his arms through the cinch straps. Mustering every scrap of his dwindling strength Iron Eyes walked towards where he had seen the trio of outlaws taking refuge.

Suddenly more shots rang out along Main Street.

Each bullet hit the well-padded saddle and rocked the tall bounty hunter but Iron Eyes refused to stop his advance. His long, skinny legs took him back to the relative safety of the buildings on one side of the street. A few more shots came out of the black alleyways. Each of them hit the saddle hanging before the bounty hunter.

Iron Eyes staggered as the impact rocked him. Without even aiming Iron Eyes blasted one of his trusty Navy Colts in answer. His narrowed eyes watched as the lead from his six-shooter carved a route through the still night air and caused windowpanes to shatter.

With dogged determination he pressed on.

Nothing could stop him now. He watched as the three shadowy figures raced further away from the cover of one building to the next.

Iron Eyes walked on.

Only death could stop him now.

10

The deafening sound of gunplay grew louder and louder. Every corner of Lobo rocked as Sheriff Lomax White hid inside his small, unlit office. He knew that Iron Eyes was in deadly peril but he simply would not risk his own hide to save anyone. The sound of the constant firing of guns rocked the small office set halfway along the wide street, and grew louder as the outlaws were forced deeper into the settlement's narrow alleyways.

A stray bullet shattered one of the windowpanes close to where the lawman was hiding but still he did not move. It was as though every nightmare which had tormented the elderly sheriff's dreams had suddenly become reality.

He held on to his scattergun tightly. His index finger curled around its large twin triggers but he was helpless to do anything.

A sickening thought came to the lawman as he shook with each shot that rocked the office. What if he were more of a hindrance than a help to the gaunt bounty hunter? He stared down at his wide girth and nodded to himself. He was a considerably wider target than the intrepid Iron Eyes.

Even soaked in the sweat of terror White wanted to go and help. Yet men like Iron Eyes seemed to like to tackle their enemies alone.

Iron Eyes was like a dog with a juicy bone. He wanted to chew on it by himself. The outlaws were his. The lawman inhaled and raised his head just above the blotter on his desk. His baggy eyes could see nothing outside except the cloud of acrid gun-smoke which grew as dense as fog beyond the window.

Iron Eyes refused either to want or permit assistance from anyone, no matter who they were. White had locked the office door when the shooting had started. The sheriff had taken refuge behind his solid desk and remained cowering there.

His aged hands clutched his scatter-gun across his chest and yet he seemed unable to move a muscle. He was terrified. In all his days in office he had never felt quite so afraid as he did now. White was out of his depth and he knew it. He had never been so bemused as he was by these events which were happening in his normally peaceful town.

What should he do?

Should he try to help the painfully skinny bounty hunter? That was what a real man would do, but for the longest while he had felt nothing like a real man.

The battle was growing more intense.

It was as though the Devil had invaded his small town in the guise of the creature that called itself Iron Eyes. White knew that he should trust the scarred bounty hunter but something deep inside him refused to believe that anyone quite so mutilated could actually be on his side.

How could anyone who looked like Iron Eyes be anything but a bad omen? his terrified mind thought. Then he heard the boardwalk clattering.

White's head turned in fright. He listened to running boots outside his office. Whose boots were they? the sheriff wondered. Were they the boots of the outlaws or those of the maimed Iron Eyes?

He dared not raise his ancient head again to peek over the edge of his desk. White swallowed hard but there was no spittle in his dry mouth.

Sheriff White trembled as he tried to force his body up off the floorboards but no matter how hard he tried the chains of fear kept him shackled to the spot.

He was helpless.

Sheriff Lomax White lowered his fearful head and cursed his own inability to find courage when it was needed. All he could do was find even more terror.

Then another volley of shots exploded

out in the street. These were closer than all of the rest. His terrified eyes watched as red-hot tapers of lethal lead whizzed past the office window. Some of the bullets ricocheted in all directions off the wooden uprights.

Fearing for his own safety White was about to move to an even safer place inside the office when he heard the handle of his door being rattled ferociously. The aged lawman clutched his shotgun tightly as his office door was kicked violently. The entire door was ripped from its frame by the boot's savage force.

It splintered into a million fragments.

The cringing lawman listened in horror as the door crashed on to the floor of his office. White trembled with fear when he then heard the boots follow it into the dark room. The boots moved across the debris towards the place where he was hiding.

The footsteps paused but White knew exactly where the intruder was. He was standing on the other side of his desk.

Not more than three feet away.

As White huddled behind his sturdy desk he heard a chilling sound that almost took his breath away.

It was the unmistakable sound of a gun being cocked.

11

Iron Eyes was soaked in blood from his two wounds. His narrowed eyes scanned the office but it was his nose that had led him to where Sheriff White was hiding. It was the scent of terror. Burdened by the weight of the saddle the panting figure released the cinch straps and eased it off his shoulders.

'Where are you, Sheriff?' Iron Eyes whispered. 'Quit hiding and get here. Pronto.'

The bounty hunter dropped the hefty, bullet-riddled saddle on to the top of the desk and eased his coat from his tortured carcass. He laid it over the saddle and slumped on to the chair.

Staring from under the desk Sheriff White recognized the bloody spurs on the mule-eared boots and rose to his feet. He saw the grim-faced bounty hunter seated on his chair. The streetlights filtered in through the gap where the door had recently stood. White was horrified by the sight of the wounded bounty hunter.

Iron Eyes stared through his limp locks and then focused on the rotund lawman.

'Got any whiskey, old-timer?' he asked, tearing his bloody shirt from his bony frame. Again White was shocked by the bounty hunter's body. He had never seen so many scars before.

White pulled the drawer of his desk open. He dragged a near-full bottle of whiskey from it. With shaking hands he gave the bottle to Iron Eyes.

'Much obliged, Sheriff.' Iron Eyes' teeth dragged the cork from the bottle's neck. He then spat it across the room and dropped his shirt on the floor. He raised the whiskey to his lips and downed a third of the bottle's contents. 'Have you got anything to tie around my arm?'

The stunned lawman looked at the bullet hole in Iron Eyes' arm. It was bleeding freely.

‘I got me some rawhide strips,’ White suggested.

Iron Eyes nodded. ‘That’ll do fine. Get them and tie them around this damn wound.’

The lawman did exactly as ordered. He worked feverishly and managed to stem the flow of scarlet gore as he tightened the strip round Iron Eyes’ forearm.

‘What’s happening, boy?’ White managed to ask as he picked up his scattergun and searched the street for danger.

Iron Eyes lowered the bottle from his lips.

‘My plan went wrong,’ he admitted. ‘Real wrong.’

‘How bad is it?’ Lomax White moved nervously to the busted doorframe and glanced out into the street. ‘How many of the outlaws are still alive?’

Iron Eyes stood up. ‘Too many.’

The lawman stared at the bounty hunter as Iron Eyes pulled his blood-drenched coat off the desk and eased it back on to his frame. Getting any information from the bounty hunter was like pulling teeth. Iron Eyes was bathed in blood and all of it was his own. White rubbed his double chin.

'How many of the varmints have you killed, boy?' the lawman pressed.

Iron Eyes grunted with laughter.

'One.' Iron Eyes spat at the floor and then returned the bottle to his broken lips. He sucked on the whiskey before lowering the bottle once more and striding to the doorway. He pushed the bottle into the lawman's hands. His cold, bullet-coloured eyes burned out into the dark street. White watched the tall, lean man. It was like watching a beast of prey prepare for its next kill.

White swallowed hard. 'What's wrong?'

Iron Eyes did not answer. His hands swept the guns from behind the buckle of his belt. His bony thumbs dragged on their hammers. The distinctive sound of hammers locking into position filled the lawman's ears a mere heartbeat before those of the outlaw.

Bob Vagas had heard the door shattering and had come to investigate. It was the last thing the curious outlaw would ever do.

With no warning Iron Eyes pulled on his triggers. Shafts of fiery revenge burst from the barrels of the guns. The two shots lifted the outlaw off his feet and sent him flying backwards. The bounty hunter stood like a statue. His eyes studied his lethal work as Vagas landed across a hitching rail.

Iron Eyes spat in contempt at the corpse.

'Make that two,' he corrected himself as he returned the hot Colts back behind his buckle.

Sheriff White was about to take a swig from the bottle when the bounty hunter's clawlike hands snatched it from him. He watched as Iron Eyes downed the remains of the whiskey.

Iron Eyes looked around the dark office.

'What are you looking for, son?' White asked.

'I'm looking for a rear door out of here,' Iron Eyes replied. He came across a blood-soaked cigar and rammed it between his teeth. The blood trailed from the corner of his mouth as he scratched a match and drew in the smoke.

'Quick. Follow me, boy.' Sheriff White moved to the back of the building. He led the skeletal figure around a bookcase and revealed a well-hidden door. He slid the bolt free and pushed the door outwards into a lane. 'What are you gonna do now, boy?'

Again there was no answer.

The haunting figure of Iron Eyes had vanished into the gloomy back alley. White glanced back at what was left of his office. Then he followed.

12

Buffalo Jim McCoy was burning up with a mixture of anger and trepidation gnawing at his craw. The deadly outlaw thought that he had outwitted the bounty hunter when he watched Iron Eyes ride out of town. Since the shooting had erupted he had lost track of his mindless followers, but he did not give a damn about his men's safety. All he was concerned about was the payroll.

He hauled two large canvas bags behind him and rested for a few moments. The weight of the two bags was more than any one man could easily handle, but McCoy did not intend to release his grip on either of them. The fortune within the canvas bags was his only reason for leaving his life of luxury and returning to the wilds of the West.

Without the money stuffed inside the bank bags McCoy had no reason even to exist. He considered his plight.

Buffalo Jim McCoy had been chilled to the bone when he witnessed his prized black roan stallion being cut down by the deadly guns of Iron Eyes. Then, after seeing two more of their mounts being shot dead, he had grimly realized that he needed replacements badly.

McCoy had barely left the vicinity of the sheriff's office when he saw Bob Vagas blasted apart by two rods of lethal fury. The normally confident outlaw instantly knew that just getting out of town alive would be a challenge.

Crawling further away from the mayhem he tried to forget what had happened during the last ten minutes. McCoy was determined to escape with as much loot as he could. If Iron Eyes wanted him he would have to work hard for the bounty on his head.

Relentlessly McCoy edged his way closer and closer to the livery stables.

That was where he could find all the horseflesh he required to escape this devilish town.

The shooting near the centre of Lobo was frantic, yet McCoy began to think that it sounded one-sided. It did not sound as if his men were fighting with the merciless Iron Eyes but rather that they were so terrified that they were firing at their own shadows.

The exhausted Buffalo Jim slid his frame behind a wagon wheel propped against a wall and rested. He strained to haul the two canvas bags close to him. The sight of two more bags on the sand near the dead horses angered the outlaw.

No matter how hard he tried to ignore the distant bags, it was impossible.

How much more money filled those canvas bags? The question burned into McCoy's soul. They had done the hard part in robbing the bank in record time, McCoy thought. Then Iron Eyes had appeared as if by magic at the side door of the bank.

How had he done that?

How could Iron Eyes have been waiting at the side of the bank when they had made their escape? How? It made no sense to the devilish outlaw.

Was Iron Eyes possessed of some sort of mystical ability unknown to ordinary mortals? No matter how many times he tried to find an answer to his own question McCoy failed.

There was a lull in the shooting.

Dragging his two bags behind him, McCoy moved through the blackest of shadows towards the wall of the livery stable. He dropped behind a large wooden trough and stared blankly at the hefty bags.

Another question then filled his thoughts.

Was he going to try to retrieve those canvas bags from the street or was he going to leave them there? He ran a gloved hand through his greasy hair and inhaled deeply. Why should he allow others to get their hands on his loot? McCoy was torn between greed and survival.

Those extra two moneybags would mean that he would be able to live in luxury twice as long as he would if he left Lobo without them.

He pulled both his guns from their holsters and started to reload them. As each fresh bullet was pushed into the smoking chambers of his weapons the desire to risk everything and go after the pair of abandoned bags grew greater.

The brooding outlaw no longer thought about the men he had hired to help him pull off this job. He did not even consider Iron Eyes.

All Buffalo Jim McCoy could see were those two bloodstained bags lying on the road beside the dead horses upon which his men had failed to reach him.

His hands expertly snapped shut both revolvers. McCoy returned one to its holster whilst he held on to the other.

Buffalo decided he was not going to leave town without all of the money he and his cohorts had stolen from the slumbering bank. They contained too much money to be abandoned, he thought. He scooped sand and piled it over the bags beside him. The bags would be safe behind the trough until he returned, he told himself.

Buffalo Jim McCoy rose to his feet and inhaled the scent of gunsmoke as he jumped over the trough. There was a fiery determination in the eyes of the deadly outlaw.

Back in the centre of town the shooting had started again but McCoy was not headed there. He used every shadow to his advantage as he advanced down Main Street towards his target.

In the middle of the wide street the two abandoned bags awaited anyone with the guts to get them.

Buffalo Jim McCoy had the guts.

13

The very centre of Lobo was filled with dense gun-smoke. Stacy Doyle and Denver Short fired their guns as they rested with their backs pressed against one another. They were shooting blindly at shadows just as Buffalo Jim McCoy had imagined. Neither outlaw was willing to allow even the merest of imagined movements to escape their lead.

'Where in tarnation is he, Denver?' Doyle shouted out above the deafening noise of their guns.

'Who is he?' Short asked fearfully.

Both outlaws ran feverishly for the cover of the saloon porch. When they reached it they leapt up on to its boardwalk. Doyle smashed a fist against the saloon's locked front doors. He glanced at Short. Both men silently cursed the fact that the Longhorn, like every other drinking hole in Lobo, was closed for business. Ducking bullets had made them both thirsty. They were like scared cats. Their eyes darted at every passing ball of tumbleweed as if it were an enemy. They toyed with their guns anxiously as they each settled beside the uprights at either end of the long porch.

With half of the streetlights shot out the long thoroughfare seemed almost eerie as clouds of smoke drifted on the night air. The smell of constant shooting was almost sickening, and they knew it had not yet stopped. The only recognizable thing bathed in starlight was the corpse of Bob Vagas, lying a few buildings away from where they stood.

They looked at it.

It was an omen of what awaited them.

Even the light of a thousand stars could not conceal from either man the brutal accuracy of the outlaw's destruction. The dead outlaw had been cut nearly in half by two lethal shots.

Vagas seemed frozen in time. The two bullets had not just ended his life, they had somehow turned him into a statue.

'Bob never had a chance,' Short spat out as he shook the hot casings from his gun and frantically searched for fresh bullets along the back of his belt.

'He did,' Doyle argued. 'He had the chance to make off in the other direction, but Bob was always a damn hothead.'

'He's a dead hothead now,' said Short, and he exhaled.

Stacy Doyle shook the spent casings from his gun and his fingers groped his gunbelt for fresh ammunition. He glanced at his cohort fearfully.

'Do you reckon that we've bin fighting with this Iron Eyes varmint, Denver?'

Short snapped his rotating chamber back into the heart of his six-shooter and cocked the hammer. He raised it to his shoulder. Only the shadows protected anyone in Lobo this night.

'Well, there seems to only be two of

us left, don't there?' Short replied. His eyes darted nervously at the slightest of movements in Main Street. 'I don't know who else can kill and not be killed. Do you? By my reckoning it has to be Iron Eyes.'

Stacy Doyle was troubled.

'I reckon you're right,' he replied.

Denver Short ran along to where his fellow outlaw was standing. He was breathing hard when he arrived.

'He's gotta be around here someplace. I sure wish he'd show himself so I can blow his damn head off.'

Doyle gave a nod. 'Maybe he is around here and maybe he ain't. I ain't too sure I want to find out which.'

Short moved closer to his fellow outlaw. He frowned.

'What you talking about, Stacy?'

'Folks die when they run up against him.'

'Yeah, they sure do.'

The younger of the pair swallowed hard. The gleaming barrel of his gun swayed in the starlight as its master continued to search for their elusive adversary.

'What if he's a ghost, Denver?' Doyle suggested. 'What if we've bin hunting a damn ghost?'

'A ghost?'

Doyle gave a long nod. 'That's what I said. What if we're fighting with a critter that ain't even alive? How can we beat a bastard like that? Maybe all them stories we've heard about him are true.'

Short was as worried as his cohort but tried not to reveal it. 'Don't talk like that, Stacy. A damn ghost couldn't fire a gun.'

Doyle grabbed Short's sleeve.

'There's just you and me left alive, Denver. How come? When we started there were five of us against one of him and now there's just two of us still living.'

Denver Short looked around the street. 'We don't know for sure that Buffalo Jim's dead, Stacy. He might be out there somewhere, stalking Iron Eyes.'

'You're fooling yourself, Denver. Buffalo's dead,' Doyle whispered. 'So are Bob and Tom. They're all dead. Just like you and me will be in a few minutes. We'll both be in Hell before sunrise. Mark my words, Denver. We're as good as corpses.'

'A man ain't dead until they put the pennies over his eyes, boy,' Short protested.

'There ain't no pennies over Bob's eyes, Denver.' Doyle pointed his six-shooter. 'I knew we were plumb crazy to hook up with Buffalo. Now we're gonna die.'

'We ain't gonna die.'

'But where's Iron Eyes?' Doyle said as he became more anxious. 'Why don't the varmint show himself?'

The older of the two outlaws had heard enough. He hauled his sleeve free of his companion's frightened grip and walked to the edge of the building. He glanced through the low-hanging clouds of gunsmoke into the darkest of lanes.

'You can wait here to meet your Maker, Stacy. I've got me a long-legged, skinny critter to kill,' he snapped.

Doyle turned his head to face his pal. His action was too slow. He raced to the edge of the boardwalk and looked vainly in all directions.

Denver Short was nowhere to be seen.

Suddenly the sound of two boots landing on the boardwalk behind Doyle drew his attention. The outlaw swung on his heels and stared at the ominous figure standing at the opposite end of the porch boardwalk.

The bounty hunter stood motionless. Every one of the stories he had heard about Iron Eyes flashed before him. Doyle squinted hard, then he began to realize that he was within spitting distance of the very man he had just been talking about. A sense of bravery swelled the young outlaw's chest as he squared up to the figure.

Sweat ran down the outlaw's face,

defying the cool breeze that moved through Lobo. Stacy Doyle held his gun against his right leg. Every fibre of his being twitched as he somehow managed to take a step forward.

'Close enough,' Iron Eyes rasped.

Doyle instantly halted.

He stared at the strange figure. In all his days he had never before set eyes upon anything quite as hideous as the bounty hunter. A thought occurred to the outlaw. If he were to kill the legendary bounty hunter, he realized, his share of the bank-robbery loot would be enough to last him a life-time. In some men courage and greed are often identical.

Iron Eyes walked two steps forward, then paused. The light from a lantern across the wide street cast its illumination upon his unearthly form.

His long mane of black hair was blowing in the night breeze. It flapped on his wide shoulders like the wings of some unholy creature.

Doyle glanced at the pair of Navy

Colts. They were not holstered but poked into the bounty hunter's pants belt. Their gleaming grips jutted out over the belt buckle. Then the outlaw remembered the gun he held in his hand. His thumb pulled back on its hammer.

Another thought came to Doyle. All he had to do was raise the gun and fire, he told himself. Iron Eyes had his guns tucked in his belt. He didn't even have a gunbelt with holsters.

'Are you the critter called Iron Eyes?'

The bounty hunter lowered his head and looked through the strands of limp hair. A cruel smile etched itself across his scarred features.

'My name is Iron Eyes,' he confirmed in a low whisper.

Again Doyle looked at the man before him. A scarecrow of a man drenched in blood. His own blood, which still dripped from his left hand as it moved down the sleeve of his trail coat. Doyle inhaled deeply. Iron Eyes' torso was covered in old scars and fresh bruises. This was no supernatural creature as legend would have him believe. This was a real man who was wounded and so skinny he looked more dead than alive. Doyle was no longer afraid. He faced Iron Eyes with a grin.

Slowly Doyle began to raise his Colt .45.

The bounty hunter flexed his fingers as his hands hovered at his sides. He took another step towards the outlaw and warned: 'I wouldn't do that if I was you.'

'You ain't me.'

Iron Eyes snatched both his Navy Colts from his belt. With brutal speed he had both cocked and fired his guns. For a brief moment he could see his target as the twin flashes lit up the porch.

The two tapers of lead had mercilessly carved their way through the darkness between the two men. The deafening roar rocked the front of the saloon as Doyle went hurtling backwards off the porch into the dust.

Mercilessly Iron Eyes looked down at the body of the outlaw. He watched as Doyle spluttered blood and his hand tried to raise and fire his gun.

The bounty hunter cocked and again fired both his pistols down at the youngster. Doyle's body arched as the lethal lead carved through him. The gun dangled on the dead man's finger before falling to the ground.

'Damned right I ain't you,' Iron Eyes muttered as he rammed his smoking weaponry back into his pants belt. 'I'm still alive.'

14

The sudden re-eruption of gunfire had taken the advancing outlaw by surprise. Buffalo Jim McCoy stopped halfway along the gap between the two buildings and knelt for a few seconds as his keen wits tried to work out where the shooting was coming from. It did not take him long to work out that the brief explosion of gunshots had come from the street he was heading towards. McCoy had used the back lanes to avoid the brutal slaughter in which he had been caught up earlier. He now summoned the remainder of his strength and moved the last few yards until he emerged from the gap between two shuttered storefronts and stared into the shadowy Main Street.

As if defying the temperature of the night air his back was soaked in sweat.

McCoy pushed the brim of his hat back. The Stetson fell on to his leather vest and dangled by its drawstring. He was anxious but still eager to reach the two discarded canvas bags.

He narrowed his eyes and peered around the area. The stars above him cast an eerie light across the town, but it was the long black shadows that gave the outlaw real cause for concern.

His eyes burned as they focused across the smoke-filled street at the front of the Longhorn saloon. No light at all reached beneath the porch overhang. It was shrouded in the darkest of shadows.

McCoy was about to continue his advance towards the canvas moneybags when he saw the body stretched out on the sand some distance away.

The outlaw felt his throat tighten as if a noose was throttling him. He drew one of his guns from its holster and held it in readiness.

Iron Eyes must have struck again, he thought.

His head moved from side to side, his eyes darting to each shadow in turn. But where was the infamous bounty hunter now?

McCoy felt as if he were reliving a much earlier exploit. A time when he had lost every one of his hired men to the venom of the bounty hunter. McCoy felt a fury deep inside him as he recalled how he had almost lost his own life to the unyielding Iron Eyes at that time. History was repeating itself. He had no idea if any of his gang were still alive. He wanted to call out to his men, but he knew that that would only draw the hunter to him.

Taking a deep breath McCoy gripped his gun firmly, raised himself up, then stared in disbelief at the quite lifeless body of Doyle.

'Damn you, Iron Eyes,' he cursed. 'Don't you know how to die like normal folks?'

He mopped up the sweat of his brow on the back of his sleeve and ventured away from his hiding-place. With calculated steps the outlaw slowly made his way into the main thoroughfare. Buffalo Jim slid like a rattlesnake into the shadows beneath the porch overhang of the feed store. Every movement now risked the danger of being shot at by the relentless bounty hunter.

He knew that his adversary could strike out unexpectedly at his chosen prey at any time. McCoy could feel his heart punching as though it were trying to escape the confines of his ribcage.

He stroked the gun with his gloved free hand. He was ready to fan its hammer and kill the demonic hunter of men. If he got the chance, that was.

Buffalo Jim McCoy rested next to the door of the store and watched the saloon opposite him. The gunsmoke still lingered on the night air. His eyes continued to dwell upon the dead youngster but there was no sign of the creature who had slain him.

Holding his six-shooter in his hand McCoy moved forward to the edge of the boardwalk.

A wooden upright and a large barrel gave him good cover but Buffalo Jim McCoy dared not relax for a solitary moment. He bit his lip. The pain kept him alert to the prospect of suddenly being caught unawares by Iron Eyes.

The bounty hunter had already proved that he had lost none of his deadly accuracy with his guns. McCoy did not want to become another notch on his gun grip.

McCoy was not a man to feel fear, but he was cautious. A decade earlier he had tasted a foe's lead and he still remembered the pain vividly.

It was not an experience he wished to relive.

His narrowed gaze darted up the street and halted upon the body of another of his men. He gritted his teeth and dropped down from the boardwalk to street level. The sight of what was left of Bob Vagas might have spooked another man but not the determined McCoy.

The array of numerous water troughs

and hitching rails that filled both sides of Main Street provided good cover right up the street to where he could see his goal.

Buffalo Jim crouched and made his way along the street in the shadows. With each step his eyes kept darting to the dead horses and the two discarded canvas bags. They were a lure he was unwilling or unable to ignore. He had worked too hard for that money just to leave it next to the slain horses, he kept telling himself.

They were his.

Not even the risk of facing Iron Eyes could deter him from getting his hands on the fortune that lay in the street.

Within a minute McCoy had reached a trough directly in line with the two bags. He paused and crouched beside the edge of the trough, his gun in his hand. The street was as silent as the grave. McCoy felt his knees begging him to straighten up but he dared not raise his head. He knew that to do so might prove fatal. His narrowed eyes searched the street but saw nothing.

There was no sign of Iron Eyes anywhere.

A cold chill traced his backbone as he paused within twenty feet of the horses and the two bulging bags. He decided to remain low to the ground as he approached the sacks of cash.

A smaller target was harder to hit. Even the legendary Iron Eyes would have trouble hitting a crouching man with his famed Navy Colts.

With no further thought McCoy moved away from the trough and kept his tall frame as small as he could. He crouched and ran for his very life towards the dead horses and the bloodstained moneybags. He made good time across the sandy street and threw himself down beside one of the stricken horses. Buffalo Jim lay stretched out in the still-warm blood of the two pitiful animals. He reached out and gripped the handles of both cash sacks and dragged them towards his prostrate form. Again his eyes darted to every dark place in search of the bounty hunter.

There was still no sign of Iron Eyes anywhere on either side of the wide street. Not a clue as to where he might be, and that troubled McCoy. His hands did not stop hauling the heavy bags until they were beside him.

Buffalo Jim rolled over in the sticky mess and glanced back at the water trough.

It was so near and yet so very far away.

A rush of trepidation filled McCoy's soul. He eased himself up on to his feet and gathered up both of the bags. He gripped their handles tightly.

He raced through the eerie starlight back to the safety of the water trough. With each frantic stride he imagined being hit by unseen bullets. To his utter surprise there were no shots. He dropped on to his knees when he managed to reach the relative safety of the trough.

Buffalo Jim McCoy was panting like a hound dog after a night's hunting.

The bags were even heavier than the others he had left outside the livery stable.

The deadly outlaw was exhausted but there was no time to rest. No time to pause. He knew that he had to keep moving and hope that Iron Eyes would not find him.

He glanced over the top of the water trough. There was still no sign of the man he knew could kill him as easily as most men could blow a match out. Iron Eyes was always dangerous even at the best of times, but there were no best of times. Every shadow posed the possibility of instant death, and that worried the outlaw.

McCoy realized that one or both of them would be dead before the night grew much older. He just did not want to be the loser.

Each grim story he had heard about Iron Eyes now seemed to be closer to the truth than even he had ever imagined possible.

Sweat flowed down his face as

though it were rain but there was no rain. There was only the ominous threat of death that seemed to lurk in every dark recess. He held the bags close to his body. McCoy swallowed hard, narrowed his eyes again and looked to the end of the long street.

All he had to do was reach the corner and the livery stables. That was where the outlaw knew he would find well-rested horses for him and his precious loot.

It was a long way to walk and doubly so when burdened with heavy bags, but the outlaw did not mean to relinquish his hold on them now. McCoy summoned up every scrap of his remaining strength and started for the corner with his bags in tow.

Every few yards he paused. There was nothing either to see or hear, but Buffalo Jim was still cautious. With Iron Eyes still on the loose it was a precaution well worth taking.

The darkness of the porch overhangs was in total contrast to the strange, eerie starlight of the street. At last, after what felt like an eternity, McCoy reached the corner. He was exhausted but he forged on towards the tall livery building.

The outlaw dropped the bags on the ground and staggered around the trough to the wall. His eyes widened in disbelief as he stared at the place where he had half-buried the first two canvas bags.

Buffalo Jim dropped to his knees and scratched frantically at the ground where he had left the bags.

They were gone.

15

The outlaw straightened up and looked in open-mouthed amazement around the area which lay close to the fragrant livery stable. It was deserted apart from the battered stagecoach, which stood close to the building's tall, imposing doors. McCoy was utterly confused. He had risked his life to get the canvas bank-bags from their resting place in the middle of the street. Now he had returned to discover that the others were gone.

Had his daring all been in vain?

The question burned into the outlaw like a hot iron.

Buffalo Jim McCoy shook his head.

'I've been robbed,' he bemoaned. 'Damn it!'

He got back to his feet and walked back to the other two bags, which he was determined not to take his eyes off.

He lifted them both off the ground and began to pace towards the livery stable's wide-open doors.

As McCoy passed the stagecoach the door of its carriage swung open and he heard the sound of a gun hammer being cocked. Every instinct for self-preservation prickled inside the outlaw.

Buffalo Jim dropped his burden and swung round, his Colt .45 in his hand. Without even aiming he squeezed the weapon's trigger as his left hand drew his back-up gun from its holster.

The area exploded into deafening action.

Buffalo Jim McCoy fired each of his guns in unison. Red-hot tapers flashed through the darkness. The door of the stagecoach was riddled with lead as the tall, emaciated bounty hunter landed on the ground.

Iron Eyes landed heavily on his wounded arm. Pain ripped through him as he saw the familiar outlaw blasting his guns wildly in his direction.

He rolled over just in time. His

dust-caked eyes saw the deep impression in the sand where he had thrown his thin frame being torn up by even more lead.

The bounty hunter raised the cocked gun in his hand and fired. Not waiting to see the results of his own shot Iron Eyes scrambled upright.

As Iron Eyes reached his full height and fired his Navy Colt a second time he felt his gun being torn from his hand by one of the outlaw's wild shots.

The bounty hunter's hand was covered in his own blood as Iron Eyes ripped his other gun free of his belt. He was about to fire when another shot cut a path through the gunsmoke and barely missed him.

Both McCoy and Iron Eyes glanced sideways into the gloom of the distant street just as another fiery taper of death came hurtling towards them.

Iron Eyes threw himself beneath the stagecoach as a lump of wood was torn from the livery stable wall. Buffalo Jim ducked inside the dark stables.

With gritted teeth the bounty hunter looked through the spokes of the stagecoach wheel and saw a figure walking towards the stable.

The man held both his guns at hip height and squeezed on their triggers again. One of the spokes was shattered. Iron Eyes ducked and was showered in choking sawdust.

He rolled over and over until he was at the front of the stagecoach. Then he cocked the hammer of the Navy Colt again and levelled the weapon at the approaching gunman.

A simple calculation flashed through the mind of the bounty hunter. As with every Wanted poster he had ever set eyes upon, every detail of it was branded into his memory. It was a skill that had proved fatal for many outlaws over the years.

Even a brief glimpse at the face told Iron Eyes everything he needed to know.

Denver Short. Wanted Dead or Alive. $600.

Iron Eyes fired his gun with his left hand. He saw the outlaw twist on his heels as his bullet caught the dangerous man in his shoulder.

To the bounty hunter's surprise and horror Denver Short did not fall. Instead the outlaw yanked hard on both gun hammers and blasted his reply.

The darkness lit up as the two rods of red-hot venom came hurtling through the night air at the bounty hunter.

Iron Eyes had only just managed to duck when two bullets embedded themselves into the fabric of the stagecoach two inches above his head. He cocked his gun again and went to fire but Denver Short had vanished. Iron Eyes wondered where the outlaw had gone when suddenly the tall stable doors were pushed wide apart.

Buffalo Jim McCoy had reloaded his weapons and was ready to strike again. He blasted both his guns furiously. The bounty hunter fell on to his knees as shots tore over his head. The side of the stagecoach tailgate was ripped apart. As

Iron Eyes tried to find cover he espied Denver Short's legs as the outlaw ascended the stagecoach.

Another shot spewed from the barrel of one of McCoy's guns.

It caught Iron Eyes' gun and ripped the Navy Colt from his hand. Now both his bony hands were bleeding. Iron Eyes turned his head and looked up at the emotionless face of McCoy as the outlaw dragged back on his gun hammers again.

Iron Eyes was unarmed. He could hear the boots of Denver Short above him. The entire stagecoach rocked as the venomous outlaw waited up on the roof for the bounty hunter to emerge.

But there was something far more pressing which gnawed at his craw. He was staring up into the barrels of McCoy's guns.

Guns which were trained upon him as the outlaw leader moved closer to his chosen target. Iron Eyes gripped the smaller front wheel and watched Buffalo Jim through its spokes.

'At long last I've got the drop on you, Iron Eyes.' McCoy laughed as smoke billowed from his gun barrels. 'Now you're gonna pay for all the trouble you've caused me over the years. You've been a thorn in my hide for too long. Way too long.'

Iron Eyes gritted his razor-sharp teeth and stared through his matted locks at the deadly outlaw. He smiled.

'You reckon you've beaten me, McCoy?' he asked. 'Didn't anyone tell you that Iron Eyes don't die easy?'

'You'll die real easy.' Buffalo Jim McCoy stopped in his tracks. A bewildered look came over his face. He raised an eyebrow and stretched his arms out to their full length. Both guns were aimed at the bounty hunter. 'What in tarnation are you smiling about? Are you loco? Don't you know when you're looking death in the face?'

There was no time to answer.

A mighty explosion suddenly rocked the area. McCoy looked to the top of the stagecoach. To his stunned horror he saw Denver Short arch his spine as he was hit by two well-placed cartridges of buckshot. Gore sprayed over the stagecoach and the sand which surrounded it. What was left of the outlaw toppled from the stagecoach roof and fell lifeless to the ground.

It crashed into the unforgiving sand. As a cloud of dust rose from around the dead body of Denver Short, Iron Eyes made his move.

With unimaginable speed Iron Eyes dragged the long-bladed Bowie knife from the neck of his boot and threw it at Buffalo Jim McCoy with all his might.

The knife flashed in the starlight as it moved through the air and somehow navigated a route between the two cocked guns held in the outlaw's outstretched hands.

McCoy gave out a hideous gasp.

His guns fell from his hands as the knife embedded itself in his chest right up to its hilt. Buffalo Jim McCoy staggered towards the stagecoach and the eyes of both men met.

'You killed me,' McCoy spluttered, blood trailing from his mouth. Before the bounty hunter could reply McCoy fell forward on to his face.

Iron Eyes crawled from beneath the stagecoach and hauled himself to his feet. There was a silence, then Iron Eyes kicked McCoy's body on to its back and reached down for the knife. His bloody hands gripped the handle of the knife and dragged it out of the body. A gruesome sound hissed from the savage wound.

'That's the first time you've said anything that makes any sense.' Iron Eyes listened as the sound of the stout sheriff walking out from the shadows came towards him.

The gruesome face of the wounded bounty hunter looked at the lawman and nodded. Smoke still billowed from the twin barrels of the sheriff's scattergun as Lomax White came to a halt beside the gaunt figure and watched the knife disappear back into the neck of the boot.

'Thanks, Sheriff,' Iron Eyes muttered. He stooped and plucked one of his guns up from the sand. 'I was wondering how I was gonna kill the bastard on the roof.'

'Is this all of the varmints, boy?' White asked.

Iron Eyes sighed. 'I sure hope so.'

White stepped over the bodies, found the other Navy Colt and returned it to the gaunt man. Iron Eyes slid both guns into his deep pockets.

'There's two more canvas bags full of money inside the stagecoach, Sheriff,' Iron Eyes muttered. He stepped on to the wheel and reached up into the driver's box. He produced a bottle of whiskey, then dropped back to the ground. 'I hid them there to confuse Buffalo.'

'I'll give you a hand with these bodies, boy,' White said. 'Help you get them back to my office.'

Looking more dead than alive the bloodied Iron Eyes shook his head and started back for the hotel. He had only taken two steps when he glanced over his shoulder back at the sheriff.

'Go to hell,' he spat. 'They're all yours.'

Finale

The following morning came early to Lobo as the blazing sun rose above the surrounding hills and spread across the sun-bleached town. Unaware of what had occurred during the hours of darkness Squirrel Sally awoke as soon as the first rays danced upon her hotel-room windows. The young female dragged on her britches and tied her oversize shirt around her perfect form. For a while she thought about nothing as she picked her Winchester up and then lifted her carrying bag. She had reached the door of her hotel room before she realized that once again she had spent the night alone.

A blazing fury hotter than the sun itself filled her very soul. Sally stopped as her hand gripped the door handle and she looked around the room for her man.

'Where the hell is he?' Sally snarled as she wrenched the door open and proceeded down the corridor towards the staircase. At the top of the stairs she paused and glared down into the lobby.

The man who had been behind the desk the night before was still there. The only difference was that he was now deep in sleep. She descended and marched across the lobby until she reached the boardwalk. Again she paused to look around the town. There were only a few of the town's early risers out on the streets as she made her way down the steps until her bare feet found street level.

Yet no matter how hard she tried she seemed unable to locate Iron Eyes. She inhaled deeply until her breasts almost exploded from their confines. She was fuming and did not care who knew it.

Where was Iron Eyes?

Why had he not returned to her as he had promised?

A sudden dread filled her young heart. What if he had ridden away?

What if he was gone?

She started to march along the street. The sand was still cool underfoot from the overnight frost. Her toes tingled with each step as she made her way halfway along the wide street.

She paused as her eyes suddenly noticed the bloodstained sand near the side of the Longhorn saloon. Sally's head tilted and her expression changed. She had seen sand stained by blood many times since she had started to travel with her reluctant companion. What if that was his blood? What if her beloved had got himself killed whilst she slept?

A chill traced along her spine. She swallowed hard.

Sally continued walking down the street.

The aromatic scent of fresh-baked bread filled her senses and suddenly she realized that she was hungry. She had walked for less than fifty yeards when she stopped in her tracks once more.

Her beautiful eyes stared down at the

churned-up sand in the middle of the street. She could see the impression left by the dead horses that had been killed there. They might have been carted away but the evidence of their fate remained.

Sally was becoming anxious and angry.

Her blonde, wavy hair floated on her shoulders as she proceeded on her way. The expression on her face was now in total contrast to what it had been when she had awoken.

Now her anger had been replaced by confusion.

Her small feet had only travelled another twenty yards when she abruptly halted. This time a terror tore at her innards. Sally glared at the ground outside the front of the sheriff's office with more than a little shock in her pained expression.

The sand was not just pink outside the lawman's office. Red traces of bloody gore still remained amid its fine granules. She felt sick as her eyes rose up and looked at the battered office.

The door had been completely kicked off its frame.

Squirrel Sally inhaled deeply and moved swiftly to the shattered door. She only stopped running when she reached the open space where once there had been a locked door.

Her eyes studied the street walls.

Chunks of wood had been riddled with bullets all around her. Her heart began to pound as she tentatively stepped into the sheriff's office and paused to allow her eyes time to adjust to the dimness within.

'Well, howdy there, little lady,' Sheriff White said from behind his desk as his large hands nursed a cup of coffee.

His voice took Sally by surprise. She dropped her bag and swung the rifle around until its barrel was aimed at the resting lawman.

Sheriff White spluttered and raised his arms. 'Easy, gal. I give in.'

Slowly Sally lowered the rifle and stepped towards the tired old man. Her eyes kept darting around his office until she had seen all of the damage that had been inflicted upon it. Her head tilted to one side as she looked into the eyes of the lawman.

'What's wrong?' he asked her.

'I was gonna ask you the same dumb question,' Sally said in a low, troubled voice. 'What you done with my Iron Eyes?'

'We had us some trouble here last night, gal,' White explained, sipping at his fresh cup of coffee. 'A whole heap of trouble.'

'What kinda trouble?' Sally pressed.

'Real bad trouble, missy,' White answered nervously. 'If it weren't for your friend Iron Eyes I reckon the miners would have lost their pay.'

Squirrel Sally levelled the rifle at the lawman again and pulled back its hammer.

'Iron Eyes ain't my friend, he's my betrothed,' she corrected.

The lawman nodded feverishly. 'That's what I meant.'

'Where is my Iron Eyes?' Sally pressed the long barrel of her rifle into the lawman's temple as she asked the question again. He lowered his tin cup and tried to smile.

'He's down at Doc Bunston's, gal,' White replied. 'Getting his wounds sewn up.'

'What?' Her expression altered again. There was panic in her face. She lowered the rifle and rested a hip against the side of the desk as she stared out through the shattered window. 'What wounds?'

White looked at her hard and long. 'Didn't you hear the shooting last night, little'un?'

Sally turned to face him. She shook her head.

'I thought that was thunder. Are you telling me that Iron Eyes got his hide shot up by some critters?'

The sheriff nodded firmly. 'Iron Eyes took on the entire Buffalo McCoy gang. He killed them all except for the one that I managed to blast to bits with my scattergun. I reckon you could say that I saved Iron Eyes' life. If I hadn't killed the varmint who was standing on the roof of a stagecoach outside the livery, that ornery varmint would have killed Iron Eyes for sure.'

Squirrel Sally looked at the lawman. Her eyes were wide and a smile played over her soft, succulent lips.

'You saved the life of my betrothed?'

'I surely did, gal,' White bragged.

She lunged at the old man again. He flinched until he felt her lips on his unshaven face. He watched as the female left his office, then he grinned.

'You're welcome, gal,' he said, touching his hat brim.

Doc Bunston's office was not hard to find. It was the only building in Lobo with a powerful palomino stallion tied up outside it. She headed straight for it.

The gun-toting female was about to march straight into the small building when the door opened. She halted her progress. Sally stared up at the awesome sight of the bounty hunter and beamed. The tall, emaciated figure stared down at his companion before brushing past her and sitting on the ground next to his horse.

Sally plonked herself down beside him and looped her arm through the crook in his.

Neither spoke for the longest time. They just silently stared at the street as more and more of the town's citizens went about their daily rituals.

At last, Sally rubbed her cheek against his shoulder and looked lovingly through her long lashes at his scarred face.

'Where's your shirt?' she asked.

He shrugged. 'Damned if I know.'

'I feared you was dead, Iron Eyes,' she admitted.

'Would that upset you, Squirrel?' Iron Eyes pulled out a cigar and placed it between his lips. His free hand searched his coat pockets and pulled out a box of matches. He slid one out and struck it. The flame rose high before being sucked into the black, twisted weed.

She nestled into him even closer. 'I guess it would. Life ain't easy for a young widow-woman in these parts.'

He shook his head and blew a line of smoke at the ground.

'You'd be my widow?' he wondered.

'Sure I would.' Sally slid her arm around his lean waist and then snatched the cigar from his mouth. She puffed on it and gazed up into his emotionless features. 'If'n you'd gotten yourself killed, that is.'

He grunted with reluctant amusement.

'Hell, Squirrel, I don't die that easy, gal.' Iron Eyes nervously wrapped his arm around her shoulder. 'After all, my name is Iron Eyes.'

'I know that.' She sighed deeply. 'You're my beloved.'

'That's mighty fine, Squirrel.' He sighed in his turn and then looked heavenwards. 'Now get your damn hand out of my pants pocket.'

Other titles in the
Linford Western Library:

STAGECOACH TO WACO WELLS

Michael D. George

Trouble is coming, and it's due to arrive on the night train into Dodge City. Marshal Ben Carter has seen gunmen gathering at the railhead, waiting for their boss to return on the mighty locomotive speeding through the wilderness towards them. The marshal knows he is no match for the deadly men gathered like vultures. It seems like time to run or die — until bounty hunter Johnny Diamond arrives, and Carter proposes they join forces . . .

WEST OF THE BAR 10

Boyd Cassidy

A group of mysterious riders is racing along the border of the infamous Bar 10 spread, determined to fulfil one mission — the killing of Johnny Puma. With his time running out, Johnny will need to rely on more than his wits if he is to face this pack of murderous strangers and survive. It's time to accept the help of his loyal friends — the famed and dangerous riders of the Bar 10.